Realms of Spells & Vampires

Fae Witch Chronicles Book 5

J. S. Malcom

Copyright © 2018 J. S. Malcom

ISBN-13: 978-1722437350
ISBN-10: 1722437359

CHAPTER 1

My skin prickles, heat flaring out from my solar plexus as magic simmers within me. Not just any magic, veil witch magic, and it takes everything I have to fight against my instincts. I've never been this close to a vampire before without striking. In fact, I've never been this close to a vampire before at all.

She looks young, the girl, maybe nineteen or twenty, although her true age is impossible to guess. She has long dark hair, gray-blue eyes and pale white skin. Well, of course she's pale. She's a vampire.

The girl, Nora, watches me too, nervous and wary in this room lit by just one dim red bulb. Does she know what I am, or what it means to be a veil witch? I'm not sure yet what she knows, so I listen as she tells her story.

"I was just coming home when I saw it, this strange light out by the street. It blinded me at first and, for a moment, I thought I'd misgauged the time. Like maybe the sun was rising, but that didn't make sense. I knew it was nowhere near morning yet."

She speaks softly, as if afraid of being heard. Or maybe thinking of that moment brings back fear. After all, to a vampire, light can mean death. Nora's eyes leave mine as she glances at Beatrice, but then her gaze returns to me. She can feel my magic somehow, I can tell. I've always wondered if they could.

As if to break the spell between us, Beatrice says, "Then what happened? We need to be sure of every detail."

Nora nods. She swallows. This isn't easy for her.

"The light, it… shimmered, I guess. It was sort of pulsing." Her eyes flick between the two of us again. "At least it seemed that way to me. I'd never seen anything like it before, so I hid behind a car. I didn't know what to do. I just—"

Nora blinks rapidly, her eyes glistening. She reaches up to wipe away a tear just in time, and I can't help but notice that it's tinged with red.

Beatrice reaches out to touch the back of her hand. "It's okay, Nora. You're safe now."

Meanwhile, I stare, part of me shocked. I've never imagined seeing a vampire cry. I wasn't sure they could.

Nora nods again, but she doesn't speak.

"Then what happened?" Beatrice prompts her, slowly withdrawing her hand. Maybe because Nora's skin is too cold?

"I saw two men. They stepped out of that light and then it closed behind them. Almost like a doorway. It got dark again, but I could still see them."

"Because you're a vampire." I don't mean to say it with an edge to my voice, but it just comes out that way. Like I resent that vampires can see in the dark.

Nora's gaze cuts to me again. "Yes, because I'm a vampire."

There's no apology in her voice, but no arrogance either. It's just a fact. She's a vampire, so get over it.

Beatrice glances at me, just briefly, but enough to convey her annoyance. She's right. I make a conscious effort to control myself, to withdraw my magic so I'm less agitated. Time to put the claws away.

Beatrice tries again. "The men," she says. "Did you know them?"

Nora shakes her head. "No. I know who one might be, but I'm not sure. The other one, no idea."

"What did they look like?"

"One was tall, with long dark hair. That one was a vampire, I could tell." She doesn't say how she knows this. She doesn't have to. Vampires move differently than we do. More quickly, more fluidly, like they barely feel gravity. If you know what to watch for, it's hard to miss. "The other one was tall too," Nora says, "but not as tall. He had strange hair. Gray, nearly white. Almost like he was—"

"Old," I say, not realizing I was going to speak. But my heartbeat just kicked up three notches at remembering what Ian said before, back when he got that flash at Bethany's apartment.

Nora waits to see if I'm going to say more. When I don't, she continues. "Yes, but he was young. In his twenties, maybe mid-twenties. He looked to where I was hiding as they walked by, almost like he could feel me there. But then the other one, the vampire, spoke. He pointed at my house and said, 'That's where they live.' After that, he kept walking, but the other one. He—"

She stops again to wipe her eyes. Then she stares straight ahead, as if she can't look at us as she describes what happened next.

"He went into the house. I don't know how he got in—magic, I guess—but the locks didn't stop him. He just reached out and the door swung open. I saw flashes of light, and I knew something terrible was happening. But I didn't do anything. I was too afraid. I just stayed hidden until after he was gone."

She doesn't try to stop the tears now as she relives that moment, in which her friends, those she thought of as her family, perished. I can't help but think about the fact that they died at the hands of someone like me.

A few moments pass before Nora resumes her story, her voice barely above a whisper. "When he finally left, I went inside, but it was too late. They were already… gone. I should have done something. I should have at least tried. Instead, I just—"

Her words cut off, her gaze still distant. She's no longer speaking to us as she admonishes herself for not taking action. Even though she wouldn't have stood a chance. Not against a veil witch. Somehow, that part still seems impossible, although I have to accept that it's the only explanation. There's another veil witch out there, one who for some reason has set his sights on me and my sister. All of his actions point to that.

At the same time, I think we've gotten as much as we can from Nora. She looks tired, her skin even more pale than before. She has dark circles beneath red-rimmed eyes. Even as I feel bad for her, I can't help but wonder when she last fed. To still have that even slight blush of blood to her skin, it can't have been long.

Beatrice looks up to where the closed-circuit camera is mounted at the ceiling. She nods and the door at the back of the room clicks open. The man who enters is named Ellis, and he looks to be around thirty. He has dirty blonde hair and kind brown eyes. He's also Vamanec P'yrin, one of those working with the Shadow Order. Beatrice told me that when he sensed the breach in the veil—something only the Vamanec P'yrin can do—he went to investigate. That's how he ended up at the crime scene. There, he found Nora trying to hide and convinced her to come in.

Now he approaches her where she sits and places his hand on her shoulder. He speaks softly. "Come, get some rest."

Nora rises from the table and I assume that's it for now, but then she turns when she gets to the door, fixing her attention on me. "We need to prove who did this," she says. "We need to make them pay."

I nod slowly, keeping my eyes on hers. Then I utter words I never imagined speaking on behalf of dead vampires. "They'll pay, believe me."

A few seconds pass as Nora stares at me hard, as if wondering whether to trust me. I can't say if she understands that I'm magically wired to annihilate threats, although I suspect she knows. Such are the rules of the supernatural world. Just as it's her fate to live as a nocturnal parasite.

"Meet me at Capital Trail and Stancraft," she says. "Ten o'clock."

I have no idea where that is, but she says no more before following Ellis through the door. Somewhere in this building, there must be a dark room where someone who's neither dead nor alive can be alone and feel safe. In other words, a room meant for a vampire.

CHAPTER 2

I run up the stairs to Autumn's apartment, having come as soon as she called. I've been up since five and my nerves are jangly from anger, anxiety, fear and worry. And, of course, way too much caffeine, but it wasn't like I could eat or go back to sleep after getting home. In other words, I'm a mess.

Autumn, on the other hand, seems calm as she lets me in. She closes the door and gives me a hug. "Hang on," she says. "I need to feed Louie."

I follow her into the kitchen, where her one-eyed cat waits by his bowl. There's a dead bird beside him on the floor. Now I understand the urgency, since it's part of their arrangement. Louie brings Autumn food in the form of dead animals, and she returns the favor by opening a can of Friskies. Strange, but who am I to comment on relationships?

Autumn fills Louie's bowl and sets it on the floor. She runs her fingers down his back. "There you go, boy."

She picks up the dead bird, wraps it in a paper towel and sets it aside. Sometimes, she brings those gifts back to life, or at least she has in the past. I haven't thought to ask lately.

Louie makes no move toward his bowl. Instead, he glowers at me through his one eye.

Autumn surprises me again, this time by laughing. "Looks like he hasn't forgotten your potion."

Right, my failed attempt at an energy potion. I spilled a few drops, which Louie lapped up. Yes, he definitely got energy, made evident by the fact that he spent hours running in circles, and then the rest of the day humping the armrest on Autumn's sofa.

"I made coffee," Autumn says. "Want some?"

"God no." I stare at her with my head cocked, wondering if Beatrice could have been wrong. Autumn seems so calm, like nothing even happened. "You said to wait until I got here. So, I'm here. What the hell happened, who did it, and how do we kill them?"

Autumn glances at Louie again, who still hasn't moved. "Come on," she says, and walks toward the living room.

Autumn flops down onto her sofa and gestures to the love seat. "Sit," she says.

I stare at her for another moment, then do as I'm told. "Okay, so tell me."

Autumn nods, but starts with a question. "How did you know?"

Shit, when she called I didn't even think about faking it. But she hadn't said anything, had she? She called, I flipped out and here I am, after breaking every speed limit in town. I sigh and say, "Beatrice told me."

"Beatrice," Autumn says. "Who's Beatrice?"

Her gaze is cool, her tone a little hard. Fair enough. I've held out on her so many times that I'm starting to forget which parts I omit.

So, I just say it. "She works at the Shadow Order. She knew Grayson. I've sort of been working with her." None of which makes sense, of course.

Autumn perches forward. "You mean Grayson who wasn't Grayson?"

I nod and say, "Right, that Grayson."

"What the hell is the Shadow Order?"

At any other time, I'd probably laugh. Even now, I could swear a smile tugs at Autumn's lips at that name.

I sigh again. "It's an organization. Secret, I guess. They're witches who investigate magical crimes. Well, not just witches. There are vampires and werewolves too. And some Vamanec P'yrin, apparently."

Autumn's eyebrows shoot up to her hairline. "And you've been working with them? What does that mean, ex—"

"Not so much working with them as trying to find stuff out. To help Bethany. At least that's where it started. Then I ended up on this team. Sort of. At least, we're training together."

Autumn appears at a loss for words. She just keeps blinking at me.

I let out yet another sigh, sounding exactly like what I am sometimes. An idiot kid sister who keeps jumping in blindly. "Sorry, I probably should have told you. I just figured I would when—"

"When, what?" Autumn says, this time cutting me off. "When you get poisoned with belladonna again?"

Okay, so I sort of forgot about that time, which would have been the end of me if Autumn hadn't installed that tracking app on my phone. All the same, we still had words about that.

"Or when you end up imprisoned in some other realm again?"

She has a point again, actually. When I finally told her about Esras—well, most of it—I sort of had to tell her about meeting his parents too. As in, serving as Raakel's slave for a week. Again, I find myself struggling for a response. After all, I deserve this for lying to her so many times. "Sorry, I'll try to be more transparent going forward."

Autumn stares at me, making me squirm.

"I promise," I say.

Crap, I really didn't want to make that promise. I just don't operate that way. At least I didn't until now.

"Okay, good," Autumn says. "We'll get back to Beatrice and the Shadow Order thing later." She frowns at me and adds, "Really? The Shadow Order?"

I shrug. "For real."

"Damn," Autumn says. "That's like something out of a cheesy movie. You didn't just make that up?"

I unzip my jacket, only now realizing that I'm starting to roast. Probably due to guilt, but still. "I don't think I even could make that up."

"Yeah, probably not." Autumn relaxes back into the sofa, crossing one leg over the other. She glances toward the kitchen, where behind me I hear Louie chomping away. A soft smile spreads across her face as she watches her damned cat. God, I love my sister.

Autumn shifts her attention back to me. "So, here's the deal. Remember when we last spoke?" Her cheeks flush a little, and I get why. At the time, she had a pretty good buzz going. "After that, I went to bed. I woke up somewhere else entirely. At first, I thought it had to be a nightmare."

This time it's me who perches forward. "Where?"

Autumn shakes her head. "I'm not sure."

I keep my eyes on hers to be sure she's not still trying to keep me from marching out there and killing someone. She's not lying, I can tell.

Autumn continues. "All I know is that it was dark, my hands and legs were tied, and—"

"What the hell?" I nearly jump out of my seat.

"Please," Autumn says. "Let me finish."

I suck in a deep breath, trying to calm down. "Okay."

"It was dark, and I was in some room with just a few candles burning. Well, I guess they were candles. They were flames, floating at the ceiling. Like I said, at first I thought I was dreaming. And then—"

"That *bitch!*" I meant to let Autumn keep speaking, but it just comes out. Yeah, I know where she was. Or at least who she was with. But then I already knew that, didn't I? Still, it's got Sarah Wellingsford written all over it.

"Can it wait?" Autumn says.

This time, I see how hard this is for her. We're past the point where it's about me, and Autumn was clearly humiliated. Right now, I need to keep my thoughts to myself. I nod and say nothing.

Autumn takes a deep breath too. "So, there were others there. Witches, obviously, but they wore Venetian masks." Seeing my confusion, she adds, "The kind that just cover your eyes. They took some blood and—"

I jump to my feet. *"They took your fucking blood?"*

Autumn glares and I drop back down.

"They took blood, enacted some sort of spell, and then it happened." She looks away. "They took my magic. They call it a binding."

It takes everything I have to contain my rage, which I just barely manage. It must be killing her, what they did. I can't even imagine. "I know. I wasn't sure if it was really a thing."

"It's definitely a thing," Autumn says. "Then they told me what I'd been accused of, they blew some powder in my face, and…" She gestures to our surroundings. "I woke up back here again."

I can't help it. I'm just curious. "Powder?"

Autumn shrugs. "Yeah, a powder. It carried a spell of some sort, I guess. It must have."

"We need to learn how to do that." I keep my eyes evenly on hers.

Autumn catches my meaning. "Yeah, we do."

"And we will," I say. "You can bank on it. It was Wellingsford. You know that, right?"

Autumn hesitates. "Yeah, it was. I wasn't sure if you knew."

So, she did know, but she was trying to protect me again. From what? Is she afraid I can't handle that old bitch? Because I can totally handle her. I swear to God if she—

Autumn's eyes remain on mine. I sigh and say, "I'll tread carefully. I promise."

"Good."

I almost can't bring myself to say it, but I have to. "I heard there's going to be trial."

Autumn nods. "In five days."

Oh, my God. *Five days?* I don't know what I expected, but I figured there'd be more time. I try to keep my panic from showing. "So, we have a little time to figure this out."

"A little," Autumn says, making me wish I'd phrased it differently.

She turns as Louie jumps up onto the sofa, and then into her lap. He glares at me, but then closes his eye as Autumn starts to pet him.

Autumn looks at me again. "You'd look after him, right?"

The question takes me completely off guard. Tears suddenly prick at my eyes as I realize what she means. She's managed to remain so calm, but I realize that's been for my sake. As always, Autumn thinks of me first. And, yes, even her cat.

"It won't come to that."

"I know it won't," Autumn says. "I didn't necessarily mean this time. Just, like, if something ever happened. I never thought to ask before."

I see what she's doing, but it still works. Damn, she's good. "Of course," I say. "As long as you take care of my snorfler."

Autumn laughs. "You have one of your own now?"

"Just a matter of time. And it's seriously not going to come to that. I mean it."

"I know," Autumn says. "Because you're going to catch him, aren't you?"

She means the other veil witch, of course, and there's no point in lying. "You bet your ass I am," I say. "And then I'm going to figure out what Wellingsford's game is. And then I'm going to take her down too."

"And it wouldn't matter if I told you that you might be up against more than you can handle. It wouldn't matter if it might be the very thing that kills you."

Finally, Autumn has started to lose control. When it was about her, she could handle it, but now her eyes glisten. I'd like to tell her that I've never needed her help before, that I'll be just fine, but that's not true. If it wasn't for Autumn, I wouldn't be here. She grew up trying to save me. It was all she thought about. And then she did it.

I feel a tear run down my cheek. "You're right," I say. "It wouldn't matter."

Autumn pets Louie for a few more moments before raising her eyes to mine again. "That's what I figured. So, about that transparency thing…"

Again, there's no point in lying. Not anymore. "There's this vampire," I say. "Her name is Nora. I'm meeting her tonight."

"Oh, shit," Autumn says.

CHAPTER 3

By the time I get home, I'm somewhere between steely resolve and blubbering breakdown. Autumn did her best at putting on a brave face. Way better than I'd be able to pull off under the same circumstances, which would probably involve a combination of screaming tantrum and ice cold terror. All the same, she knows what she's up against. That knowledge showed in the dark circles beneath her eyes. I heard it in the almost defeated tone of her voice. She seemed almost resigned to her fate. Not like she's given up, but more like she knows the fight is now out of her hands.

Which is essentially true. She's been cut off from her powers while this fight is all about magic, soon to take place on a magical battlefield. I can barely imagine what it would feel like to be violated that way. Magic just becomes so much a part of who you are. Even when you're not using it, you know it's there—that power source at your core, that force you know will be there when you find yourself in danger. To find it suddenly gone is nearly incomprehensible.

Ironically, my own magic simmers close to the surface, setting my skin to prickling. I want nothing more than to light up an orb, to let electricity crackle at my fingers, but Autumn's right. I need to be patient and careful. I need to find out who's behind what we're facing and why they're doing it. Then and only then will I be able to kick some serious ass.

I climb the stairs to see Wendy and Alec standing just outside Wendy's door. The same door which just last night I blew off its hinges. Speaking of magic, I can only assume some was involved in repairing the damage I did. Either that, or a crapload of wood glue.

I'm almost at my own door when Wendy and Alec break off conversation. She makes eye contact. Well, maybe Alec tries too but I don't look at him. Either way, it appears that this isn't the time to try slinking into my apartment to either have a good cry or blow out the windows. Probably for the best, actually. Neither will do me any good.

I go to them, keeping my focus on Wendy. "How are you feeling?"

She offers her usual smile, as if she doesn't have a care in the world. "Good," she says. "I have my reiki class soon. Want to come check it out?"

This isn't the first time Wendy has invited me, so it won't be the first time I pass. I figure I'll leave energy healing to those with personalities more suited to the task. I'm afraid I might break someone.

"Maybe not today," I say. "Got a second to talk?"

The smile almost leaves Wendy's face. "Sure, what's up?"

What's up? She nearly got devoured by the portal equivalent of the mouth of hell. "Well, I was wondering what you might remember about what happened."

Wendy shrugs. "Not much, really, but Shakeesha enhanced all of our wards this morning. I'm sure it won't happen again."

Okay, so maybe our building manager, Shakeesha, fixed the door too. Although, I have serious doubts about any wards working against whoever created that trap for Wendy. All the same, right now I need to learn as much as possible.

As much as Wendy hates focusing on the negative, I try again. "Do you mind telling me what you saw?"

"Not at all. Mostly, just a butterfly garden."

"Butterfly garden," I say. Why doesn't this surprise me?

"Like I told Alec, I went into my apartment but found myself in a butterfly garden. It was just like a place I went to with my parents when I was little. The thing is, it felt like I was seeing it then again too. I felt just like a little kid. I thought I'd somehow managed to manifest it from my memories."

Not exactly, but it sure looks like *someone* did. "And that's it? You didn't see anything else? Or maybe *anyone* else?"

Wendy shakes her head. "Nothing like that."

"So, you never felt you were in danger?"

"Not at all. At least not until you grabbed me. Then it was like I woke up from a dream."

So, she does remember me being there. I wasn't sure. Still, this is bad. Really bad. It means that if I hadn't been there, Wendy wouldn't have stood a chance. No wonder the others got taken. They probably never knew what hit them. Except for one thing. When I grabbed Wendy, she knew. So, that image of Bethany's tortured expression must have been burned into her mirror after she realized where she'd been taken. The question being where?

There's something else that bothers me. Really bothers me. The other veil witch not only knows how to open that portal, he knows how to weave traps from his victims' memories. I don't know what that is, but it definitely isn't veil witch magic.

Wendy snaps me out of it. "Well, I should go," she says. "Thank you for helping me last night. I hope all of this ends soon."

She says it like we're talking about bad weather, but I guess that's Wendy's way of dealing. She's a firm believer in the positive. She thinks that denying the negative her mental energy will deprive it of power. Maybe she's right. After all, something did come along and save her. Okay, that something was me, but still. Wendy barely experienced what happened, and there's no way I'd want that to change for her.

So, all I can say is, "Yeah, me too. I have a feeling it will."

By which I mean that I very much plan to make it end, along with the person, or people, making it happen. But that's my fate, to be a supernatural guard dog. Wendy drew a different card entirely. I wouldn't change that for her either.

Wendy walks off, throwing one last smile our way from over her shoulder. She disappears down the stairs and it's just me and Alec now standing in the hall.

"Well, I should probably get going too," I say.

Alec brushes his hair back, his blue eyes meeting mine. "Seriously?"

I gesture toward my door, pretending I don't know what he means. In other words, that I've completely ignored him.

"I have some stuff I need to take care of before—"

"I heard about your sister," he says. "I'm sorry."

I stare back at him. "We'll take care of it." I almost start walking, but then add, "What about the others? Do they know?"

Alec shakes his head. "Not yet, but I guess it's just a matter of time."

I feel that anger flare up inside me again, along with it the magic that wants so badly to get out and do damage. "So, what, it's just a matter of your connections again?"

Alec frowns. "Again?"

Right, everyone knew about the coven meeting. I lashed out at him irrationally last night. "Whatever. Like I said, we'll take care of it."

Alec nods, his unruly hair falling back down over his forehead. "Sure. I just thought I'd see if there was anything I could do. But you've got it covered, obviously."

I turn my back and start walking toward my apartment, not sure if I'm pissed off at him, the world in general, or myself. I'm about to unlock my door when Alec says, "Hey,

Cassie? You're right, in a sense. I did hear about it through my family."

I don't look at him as I insert my key into the lock.

"But that's the only part you're right about," Alec says. "Just figured you should know."

I'm about to turn to him and try offering a response, but Alec walks past me without waiting. I watch when he reaches the stairs, but he doesn't look back then either. He just keeps going.

~~~

I enter my apartment and close the door behind me, suddenly not so glad to be alone. The fact is, Alec's words hit home. Maybe right now it's good that my mirrors remain covered, because I'm not sure if I'd like what I see. Why the hell do I keep doing that around him? Is it really just because he looks like Grayson?

"I can't be that shallow," I say, muttering as I walk toward the kitchen. "I'm not, right?"

Of course, no one is there to hear me. I'm talking to myself, and it's not the first time I thought about getting a cat of my own. Aren't witches supposed to have cats anyway? Familiars, right? Another bit of witch lore I never really believed. Then again, I also thought witches couldn't fly.

As for getting a cat, I'm not sure it would work out. I tend to overdo things, so I probably have latent potential for becoming a cat lady. I'm also not sure it would be fair. Sure, the company might be nice, but what about the next time I wander off world and get drunk? What if I end up married in some other realm and forget to come home?

Whoa, where did that come from? Nice try, brain. You thought you could just sneak that one in there without me noticing, didn't you? Or maybe you wanted me to notice, because now my thoughts drift from my cat lady potential to both Phoenix and Esras. I try telling myself they have nothing to do with what's going on, but that's hardly the case. After all, saving my sister is only part of it. I need to save Bethany too. So, one way or the other, Phoenix and I will be going through this together. As for Esras, he may not be tied up in this yet, but I have a feeling he will be soon. There's just no way to ignore those demon incursions into Faerie. Also, that magic I faced last night felt way too familiar.

Which brings me full circle to those magical strikes carried out through speculomancy. I can't help thinking that particular magic was chosen because Maggie and I had recently been discussing it. So, like Maggie said at the coven meeting, it's being used to make a statement. Namely, that I've once again been secretly observed. Which also seems way too familiar, making me think that our mysterious veil witch must be receiving magical assistance. And clearly he's upping his game. He didn't slither out of a mirror to kill those vampires. That time, he came out of the veil. Which tells me he's getting stronger, bolder, and more determined. But last night showed that I can definitely fight back. If I can do that much knowing next to nothing, then I'm just getting started.

CHAPTER 4

There's a reason why the street names Nora gave me didn't seem familiar. First, because one isn't a street name. Capital Trail is a paved path down by the river following the railroad tracks. Technically, Stancraft Way is a street, but just barely. It's a lonely little stretch of forgotten nowhere, on one side overgrown with bushes and trees, and on the other occupied by just a few derelict buildings. I think. It's kind of hard to be sure, given that there aren't any streetlights. In other words, it's just where I want to be right now, having gotten off the bus and walked at least a mile alone through the night.

Then something occurs to me. *Am I alone?* I look around and say, "Nora?"

"How's it going?"

I almost jump out of my skin. She's like ten feet away and I didn't know until she spoke. Now I can just barely make out the pale blue glow of her eyes. Presumably, she's been watching me since I got here. It takes everything I have not to power up my magic. Instead, I power up my flashlight app and shine the thing her way.

She spreads a hand to cover her eyes. "Do you mind?"

"Are you for real?" I say, but I kill the flashlight app.

"Sorry, I forget sometimes."

Now it's just her voice again as I wait to regain my washed out sight. If there was ever a moment for a vampire to jump me, this is it. Then again, she could have done that already. "Forget what?"

"How blind you guys are. Then again, I can't see shit during the day. But that's due to allergies."

Actually, that's pretty funny. Good to know the vampire has a sense of humor. In that same moment, a cloud blocking the full moon drifts away. Thank you, cloud. Yes, I see her now, realizing why I couldn't before. She's wearing jeans and a dark hoodie, the hood still lowered to shadow her face.

"I see you found it okay," she says. "Sorry, it's kind of secluded."

"You might have mentioned that."

She shrugs. "You're right. I should have. I wasn't really myself at the time."

Fair enough, all things considered. "You sound better," I say. It's not like I know her, but she just does.

A beat and then she says, "I'm okay."

Two words that somehow carry so much weight. *I'm okay*, meaning I've been around a long time. I've seen some serious shit. I was once alive and now I'm not, but then again I am. And what can you do with that? I feel all of it in just her weary tone.

I don't comment on anything that just passed through my mind. Instead, I get to the point. "Why are we here?"

Nora walks closer, mostly a shadow with just those two eyes growing larger. "How do I know I can trust you?"

Damn, speaking of getting to the point. It's also a very good question, especially since I was just thinking the same thing. I decide to go with honest. "Because I need you. How's that?"

That's not enough, apparently. "And what about when you no longer do?"

I'm not sure what she's getting at, but there must be a reason she's asking. My guess is that she wants to share something, but isn't sure she should.

"How about my word?"

"To be sure, I'd have to take a look. Can I trust you not to kill me, veil witch?"

It takes a moment, but I get it. Vampires can control human minds, which must mean they can also get inside them. At least to a degree. It's one hell of a risk, but I'm not sure I have a choice. The stakes are just too high right now.

So, I take my life in my hands. "Sure," I say. "Have a look."

Her eyes grow closer, and larger, to the point where the glow of them is nearly all I can see. She steps closer yet again and then I feel it, a humming sensation settling over my brain, along with the flickering of lights at the back of my skull. Then she pulls back again. That soon and it's over, but I just learned something. The vampires came from the Vamanec P'yrin. They may have lost some of that pureness of magical strength over time, but not all of it. I think I could have pulled away on my own, but I'm not entirely sure.

"I believe you," Nora says. "Let's go."

She starts moving fast, walking down the street at a ridiculous pace. I hoof it to catch up, but it's still not enough. Nora looks back over her shoulder, then slows to a pace I can manage. "Sorry," she says. "Force of habit."

I nod, trying not to let on that I'm winded. Then again, I'm not really sure how acute her senses might be. Can she hear the accelerated beating of my heart? Smell the sweat that just broke on my forehead? My guess is yes, in both cases.

We walk for maybe half a mile, then leave the street to take an old road that's been closed to cars. These days, it's more just another path than anything. It's cracked and full of potholes, overgrown where mud has sat long enough to produce crops. At the end there's a chain-link fence topped with razor wire, behind which hulks a series of dilapidated brick buildings. There's a gate in the fence that's bound closed with chain. There's also a no trespassing sign. We go around to the back, where Nora leads me through a hole that looks to have been torn through the chain-link, reminding me of how strong vampires can be. Another reason why I usually keep my distance.

Ironically, I have to keep close to Nora. She might be able to see where we're going, but it's been touch and go for me. We stop as we approach the buildings, where Nora takes out a cell phone. She fires off a quick text.

"Just letting them know it's me." She doesn't explain who she means by "them," but I don't get to think past that when Nora says, "Okay, we're good."

She slips her phone back into her pocket and we start walking.

"What is this place?" It seems like the perfect place to follow a vampire if you're hoping never to be seen again. Or, at least if you want to make sure you never again see daylight.

"Home to some friends," Nora says. "Which is why I needed to know if I could trust you. It wouldn't exactly be okay if you came back later and reduced them to ash."

Right, I have done that to vampires a few times, so I can't exactly argue. But, from what I've gathered in the past, vampires often live in posh circumstances, having had decades, sometimes centuries to amass wealth. Very much like the Vamanec P'yrin, actually. So, why would this dump be home to any vampires?

We approach one of the buildings and I can see it more clearly now. It looks like an old factory of some sort. Even by moonlight, I can tell that the exterior is half covered with moss, while the other half is smattered with graffiti. Tall, thin openings for windows, which arch at the top, were bricked over at some point too. Probably to keep out squatters. Presumably, vampires weren't anticipated.

A door made of rusted steel groans open as Nora pushes against it. I look past that opening to see a pitch black void. Seriously?

Yes, seriously.

I follow Nora just a few steps inside before I'm completely blind. I have to stop walking.

Nora sighs. "Use your cell phone," she says.

Right, of course, but did we really need the attitude? I dig out my phone and click on the flashlight app, immediately wishing I hadn't. I'm basically in a tomb, ahead of us a steel staircase covered with cobwebs and leading to God knows where. Beyond that, there's a vast hollowed out space that must have once been a manufacturing floor. The place reminds me of the abandoned warehouse where, not long ago, I ran for my life as someone tried to kill me. Although, by comparison, the abandoned warehouse was bright and cheerful.

Nora starts climbing the stairs. No, she doesn't need to light up her cell phone. Apparently, she can see perfectly. Tell me again how I managed not being killed by vampires in the past?

"This place was once an aluminum plant," she says. "Word is it's coming down in about six months to make way for a new apartment complex."

"It's nice," I say, almost positive that a rat just scurried past on its way downstairs.

Nora chuckles. "Thought you'd like it."

We reach a landing and Nora stops. She turns to face me, causing my heart to skip a beat. If she made a move right now I'd be toast. I've dropped all of my defenses. Our eyes meet and a smile tugs at the corner of her lips. Yes, she totally knows what just crossed my mind.

"See, here's the thing about vampires," she says. "Not all of us have the advantage of belonging to a group. Some are turned and forgotten, left to scrap for themselves. It's not easy. Has that ever occurred to you?"

The answer is no, it's never once occurred to me that there might be vampires in need. The concept is just so strange, especially since I've wiped them out like cockroaches at any given opportunity. None of which I say as I keep looking back at Nora.

"That's what I thought," she says, and starts climbing again. "So, those particular vampires get into the habit of keeping their ears to the ground. They pretty much have to if they're going to survive. They also end up living in places like this for a while. Years, sometimes decades. And that's if they're lucky."

I'm not sure what to say as we ascend another length of staircase to the third floor. We stop on another landing, in front of another steel door. Nora turns to me again. "Ready to meet my friends?"

"Sure. That sounds great." In other words, should I light up an orb right now? I don't, but it's not easy. Especially since my supernatural radar just started pinging like crazy. I'd just managed to tone it down where Nora was concerned, and that took some doing. Now, all of my instincts tell me to prepare for battle.

"This should be interesting," Nora says.

She swings the door open and I prepare myself to venture further into the tomb. So what I see next takes me completely off guard. Beyond the door, there's a floor full of light, enough so that my pupils dilate. As my vision starts to clear, I see that the light comes from above, where somehow ceiling lamps have been brought back to life. The cement floor is partially covered with beat up old area rugs, beneath which electrical cables snake their way toward what looks to be some sort of rigged up power junction.

Two guys sit sharing a sofa. They're around my age, both of them holding remotes while their video game displays on an old TV. One has tawny hair and brown eyes. Even seated, I can tell he's tall. The other looks to have once had olive skin, leaving him not quite as pale as his buddy. A blonde girl sits with her legs draped across the arm of an upholstered chair. She's wearing torn jeans and a ratty old sweater. She was staring at her phone, but all three vampires look our way now. Well, they glance at Nora, but they stare at me. I swear the tall guy licks his lips.

The olive-skinned guy says, "What the hell?"

"It's okay," Nora says. "I'll explain everything. Mind if we sit down?"

Not waiting for a response, she swings the door closed and crosses the room. Heart pounding, I follow after her to where we both drop down onto another sofa. Nora pulls back her hood, runs her hand through her hair, and lets out a weary sigh. "So, obviously you heard about what happened. Now I'm trying to figure out what to do about it."

How they know, I have no idea. Maybe Nora called them?

The lick-lipper tears his eyes from me to study Nora. "How are you holding up?"

"As well as can be expected," she says.

The other guy says, "Who's the witch?"

I have no idea how he knows. Something he feels? Smells? I'll have to ask Nora later, which in itself is a strange thought.

"This is Cassie," Nora says. "She's one of the veil witches you guys heard about."

At this, their eyes go wide. The girl actually scoots back in her seat, tucking her legs up and wrapping her arms around her knees. Much better. My pulse starts to slow as I remind myself that I'm not going to be anybody's dinner. On the contrary, I hold the upper hand in this room.

Before the questions start—or possibly accusations—Nora says, "Cassie, this is Stephanie, Eric and John," indicating first the girl, then the shorter guy and finally the taller one.

Wary eyes meet mine again as, slowly, the three vampires nod. I guess they must know Nora well enough to trust her, but I can tell they're not happy.

I'm kind of at a loss, so I just give a little wave. "How's it going?"

The vampires ignore my casual question and look back to Nora. Okay, be that way.

"So, here's the deal," Nora says. "As you know, I decided to trust the Shadow Order and talk to them. It didn't seem like I had much of a choice. Anyway, that's where I met Cassie. They thought we should work together."

"Why?" Stephanie says. "She's a freaking veil witch. What makes you think she won't kill you? Or the rest of us?"

"She won't," Nora says. "She let me look."

Eyebrows are raised at that one. Maybe they figured a witch would never risk letting a vampire take control of her mind. Actually, that probably was pretty stupid. What the hell was I thinking?

"Here's what we know so far," Nora says. "Whoever killed my friends was another veil witch. None of the witches know who he is, and I'm the first person who's actually seen him. He's probably the same guy who's been killing those witches."

"They're not dead," I say. "Not yet, anyway." Even as I say it, I'm not sure how much I should tell the vampires. Although, obviously, they know at least some of what's been going on.

"Well, my people are dead," Nora says. "That's for sure."

I'm not sure what to say. After all, Bethany and the others might still have a chance. The same can't be said for Nora's friends.

Nora shifts her attention back to the three vampires. "This witch, whoever he is, was brought to my house by another vampire. Not one I've seen before, but I might know his name. Have any of you guys heard of someone named Mason?"

Stephanie lifts an eyebrow. "Guess you don't get out much."

There's an undercurrent of resentment in her tone, signaling an implication I don't understand.

"Not so much lately," Nora says. "Why, what's the deal?"

"Where did you hear about him?" Stephanie says.

Nora hesitates, then takes a deep breath as if to steady herself. "Joel mentioned him. Last week, when he was talking to Thomas. I heard him say that he and someone named Mason had gotten into a disagreement. I remember Thomas telling him to be careful."

Stephanie, John and Eric exchange glances, but none of them speak. I assume Nora is talking about her dead friends.

Nora's eyes flick back and forth between them. "What is it?"

"Mason came up from Atlanta a few months ago," John says. "Word is he's both powerful and ruthless, and that his reputation preceded his arrival."

"And that he's gained a bit of a following," Stephanie says. "We figured it might be best to steer clear."

Before that one goes unexplained, I have to ask. "Why's that?"

Stephanie's eyes meet mine, hard and flat. Evidently, she doesn't appreciate questions from the witch in the room.

"She needs to understand," Nora says, her tone telling me she sympathizes with Stephanie.

Stephanie looks from Nora to me again, her gaze just slightly less hostile. "For some of us, it's better to fly under the radar. Especially if there's going to be a shift in power."

Okay, I think I get it. Not that I've made a study of vampire politics, but I remember Autumn telling me about some dude named Phillip, who in these parts is considered to be the "arch vampire." So, basically he's the head honcho. And if there's a potential power struggle brewing, choosing sides will carry risks. Even more so, I take it, for those at the bottom of the heap.

"So, this Mason guy," I say. "What made him come up here?"

Eric shakes his head. "Good question. We don't know, but he must have had his reasons to show up all of a sudden."

The timing is interesting to say the least, and I can't exactly convince myself it's just a coincidence. I look to find out what Nora is thinking, but her eyes have grown distant. She speaks softly, as if to herself. "So that must be it. Mason set us up because of that argument with Joel."

She has to be right, of course. That disagreement must have led to Nora's friends being targeted. And somehow this Mason character had already established some sort of alliance with the mystery veil witch. Enough so that he could arrange for that witch to do his dirty work. I can't begin to imagine what brought them together, but the act served both of their agendas. In Mason's case, the settling of a score, while the veil witch magically framed my sister.

Glances are volleyed around the room while Nora keeps thinking. Even I'm included this time. Obviously, no one knows quite what to say.

Finally, it's Nora who breaks the silence. "Where can we find him?"

When she says it, I suddenly wonder if that's why she agreed to work with me. Does she think it's just a matter of me taking out Mason? I agree he has to go, but there's way more to it I'm sure. In fact, right now I need that vampire alive way more than I need him dead.

Either way, apparently it's not going to be that simple. "No idea," Stephanie says. "Like I said, we're doing our best to fly under the radar."

"But you said you've seen him around," Nora says.

Again, Stephanie shrugs. "Once or twice."

A few moments pass as Nora thinks. "Okay, well maybe we will too. I'm assuming it must be about that time for you guys. Like you said, I've been keeping pretty close to home."

"You've kind of had a steady supply," Stephanie says, her tone bordering on resentful.

Nora hesitates, and then nods. "That's true. But, come on, you would have done the same thing."

Stephanie sighs. "You're right. We would have."

"And it's not like I haven't been in the same position," Nora says. "You guys know that."

I'm not entirely sure what they're talking about. All I can guess is that lately Nora hasn't had to hunt much for her food. That's something I've heard of, that more established vampires sometimes have willing donors. Usually, humans hoping to be turned. At other times, the vampires might even have a connection with someone who can supply blood bags. But at one point it sounds like Nora must have been out there scrapping too, just like her less fortunate vampire friends.

"Still not sure it's a great idea," John says. All the same, he sets down his game controller, signaling that he might be waffling.

Nora offers him a reassuring look. "Don't worry. I won't do anything stupid."

Eric gestures toward me. "What about her?"

Nora shifts her gaze my way, her eyes lingering on mine. "She won't do anything stupid either, right?"

It takes me a moment, but I get it. They can't exactly have me following them around randomly melting vampires. "Just gathering facts," I say. "On my honor."

"And, hey," Nora says. "Can you rein in your vibe a little more? It's not like we can't feel it."

Right, that. I take silent calming breaths, forcing my magic to back off. It's not easy, but I manage to dial it down a few notches.

"Better?" I say.

Nora nods. "Better. See if you can keep that under control." She shifts her attention back to her friends. "Are we good?"

After a moment, Stephanie shrugs. "Okay fine. I'm freaking starving. Let's get moving."

CHAPTER 5

The list of things I never imagined doing keeps getting longer. Now I get to include heading out to feed with a pack of vampires. To make it seem somehow even more surreal, we take the bus. Until tonight, it never occurred to me that vampires might even ride a bus. I guess I just thought they remained lurking in the shadows until they popped out for veil witch target practice. But why not? There's no rule saying pale people with fangs can't ride the bus. Okay, technically, their fangs don't descend until they're ready to feed. Still, it's a miracle I never ended up sitting beside one before. Which I'm sure would have turned out great when I reduced my seatmate to a pile of bones.

I sit next to Nora, her at the window and me at the aisle, with Eric and John in front of us. Stephanie sits across from me, where she shares a seat with an old guy reading a book. I can't help but imagine Stephanie suddenly plunging her teeth into his neck.

I must not be too far off, because Nora leans across me to talk to her. "So, what's good these days?"

Wait, does she mean what I think she means?

"There's a new club down by the canal," Stephanie says. "I hear it's quite the smorgasbord."

Yep, that's what they're talking about. At first, it strikes me as strange that they make no attempt to lower their voices. Then again, without context, it just sounds like they're discussing options. Which, of course, they are. Meanwhile, Eric stares at his phone. From what I can see, he's reading the news to catch up on the political landscape. John listens to music through earbuds, his vampire head bobbing to some beat I can't hear. It's just so freakishly normal. No wonder people don't notice.

Before long, the bus pulls to the curb and we start filing off. My pulse escalates as I think about what lays in store. Maybe Nora hears my heart beating because her eyes gleam with amusement. "Sure you're up for this? I could always report back later."

I actually do think about bailing, but the stakes are just too high. I also pride myself on rising to a challenge. How I've lived this long is hard to say.

We mix in with people on the sidewalk, soon approaching a block lined mostly with bars and clubs. Now that we're here, I have no idea what to expect. Nor can I see how this is a feasible plan. Do they just converge on club-goers like a pack of hungry wolves?

Thankfully, that doesn't happen. Instead, we circle the block and then another, repeatedly venturing further out and then back in again. The vampires chat and banter the entire time. They trade stories. They goof off and laugh. At first I'm not sure what they're doing, but I finally realize the method to their madness. It may not seem like it, but they're hunting. It's just that they can see, hear and smell things undetectable to me. Their behavior is the perfect camouflage. What deer hunter wouldn't look, sound and act just like a deer if he could? In a way, it's terrifying to think how perfectly disguised vampires are, at night virtually indistinguishable from anyone else. No wonder humans keep failing to wipe them out.

Another factor is time. Like all immortal beings, time moves differently for vampires. This becomes more evident as an hour passes, and then another, my companions seemingly oblivious. It keeps getting later, with fewer people on the streets, which at first I think must be a disadvantage. But then I remember the times I've been accosted by vampires. It's always been late, and I've almost always been alone. So, it could be that this is a waiting game to isolate prey.

We're almost back to where we started when Stephanie abruptly stops. She cocks her head, listening to something I can't hear. Then she nods to the others. We shift direction and cross the street. We cut into an alley. It's only when we're between two buildings, and all the other street sounds fade, that I too hear her voice.

"Hey, it's Jenny," she says. "Where did you guys go?" She sounds confused, alone and a little scared as she talks into her phone. After a moment, she says, "I just needed to get out of there for a while. When I came back you guys were gone. Call me, okay?"

As a group, we suddenly stop, remaining out of sight to the person we hear. The vampires exchange eye contact in a moment of silent conference. Then John whispers to Nora, "You stayed at that place last night, right?"

She whispers back, "Yeah, but that's okay. I'll—"

"Go," Stephanie says. "We can wait."

Nora hesitates one last moment, and then starts walking, her footsteps silent against the pavement. A moment later and she's gone, having blended into the shadows. The others fall back.

Now, I'm faced with a dilemma. I can fall back too and pretend this isn't happening, or follow Nora to stop it. I know I signed onto finding Mason, but standing by like this goes against all my instincts.

I set myself in motion but it's already too late. Nora holds onto the girl, one arm wrapped around her waist and the other supporting her back. The girl's legs have buckled, her head hanging back as she lets out helpless moans. Magic surges within me, my hands prickling with electricity, but then I remain rooted to the spot. Partly because I'm not sure what I'd do. I only know one way to handle vampires, and I can't do that to Nora. Then I realize that those sounds I hear are moans of pleasure.

Nora keeps her mouth pressed to the girl's neck, her throat working to suck in blood. By the light of the moon, her eyes meet mine. They glow pale blue, but not with the savage hunger I expected. Instead, I see that she too is experiencing pleasure, both sensual and unexpectedly intimate. Within me, the urge to kill suddenly shifts to a feeling of awkwardness. Like I just walked in on two people having sex.

While I know vampires control minds, I always assumed their victims felt helpless terror. This is something else entirely, and my discomfort grows as Nora's victim switches from moaning to panting, the pace of her breathing becoming more rapid. Do the other witches know about this? Why hasn't anyone told me?

A few more moments pass before the girl emits another sound, this time the soft cry of climax. Then I hear Nora whisper, "You liked that, didn't you?"

"Yes," the girl says softly. "Can we do it again?"

Nora chuckles "Not tonight, babe. It wouldn't be good for you."

"Please?"

Nora gently shushes her and the girl says nothing more.

"Come on, let's get you home," she says. "Where do you live?"

They walk past me, the girl shuffling while Nora keeps her from staggering. I have no idea how drunk she might have been to begin with, but that's the impression now. Nora appears as one friend helping another. I follow after them, catching up as they reach the street. Nora keeps her arm around the girl, who rests her head on Nora's shoulder. Nora keeps stroking her hair.

"Do you mind hailing that cab?"

It takes me a moment to realize that Nora is talking to me. I didn't think she even knew I was there. I look down the street to see the cab parked at the end of the block. I shine my flashlight app, clicking it on and off a few times. The car pulls forward, soon stopping in front of us.

"Here, hold onto her for a moment."

I turn, thinking I must have heard wrong, but Nora shifts the girl to me. Suddenly, I'm hanging onto a hundred and twenty pounds of dead weight. It takes everything I have not to spill both of us to the sidewalk. Thanks so much, Nora.

The cab driver rolls down his window. "Who's going where?"

Nora approaches the car and speaks in a steady, firm voice. "Please listen closely. You will take my friend to three-forty-one Tyburn Street. You will help her get inside. You will not touch her or hurt her. Do you understand?"

Damn, the mind control vibe coming off of her is so strong that even I can feel it. I have to shake my head to regain focus. Then I hear the cabbie say, "Sure, of course. Three-forty-one Tyburn. Help her get inside."

"And what else?"

"Don't touch her or hurt her. I'd never do that."

Maybe that part's true. I'd like to think so, but it's clear the cab driver has been seriously mesmerized. Meanwhile, Nora motions for me to assist the groggy girl into the cab. I get her seated in back, lift in her legs and shut the door. The girl stares at me blankly through the window.

I hear Nora whisper, "Got any money?"

Boy is she asking the wrong person. I haven't had a cleaning job since booting Dorothy the Drunk from Martha Sanders' house. "Not much," I say.

Nora turns back to the cabbie. "You already got paid, okay?"

"Sure," he says. "I already got paid."

"Big tip too."

"Big tip. Got it. Thanks."

"No problem." Nora pats the roof of the cab and says, "Off you go now."

We watch as the cab drives along a now empty street. Soon, it turns a corner and disappears. Just another vampire victim being driven home by a mesmerized cabbie. If nothing else, the supernatural world never gets old.

A second later, I jump at the sound of Eric's voice close to my ear. "Guys, I don't think we're alone."

I spin around to see that both John and Stephanie stand beside him. I look to where Eric is pointing and my already escalated pulse ratchets up another notch. Down the street, a figure just emerged from an alley. I don't have to get any closer to know that it's a demon.

CHAPTER 6

My first instinct is to run like hell and just keep running. It's not that I'm afraid of demons. At least, usually I'm not, but even from a distance I can tell this fucker is huge. I have just seconds to think about the timing, and whether it could possibly be a coincidence. I sure as hell hope so, or my cover is already blown.

The demon starts to advance, and by advance I really mean charge. It's a bull of a creature, barreling toward us on all fours. If there's anyone still inside those clubs around us, I hope they're locking their doors tight.

Eric falls back, followed by John and Stephanie. Nora alone remains by my side. Damn, she's a brave little thing. Or maybe she's still blood drunk from that little cross between a soft porn and a late night meal.

"What the hell is that thing?" she says.

Okay, maybe she's just frozen with terror. If anything can kill a vampire it's coming at us fast.

"Demon," I say.

"Yeah, obviously. What kind of—"

That's as far as she gets before the demon slides to a stop before us, a cloud of smoke rising into the air. Along with that comes the acrid smell of burning tar. Apparently the thing burned up the road along the way.

I wasn't wrong about it being huge, when I was hoping that might have been an optical illusion. On all fours it's massive, but then it rears up onto powerfully muscled legs. The creature has to be eight feet tall, with a flat head and two slits for eyes glowing fiery red. Corkscrew horns protrude from its forehead.

"Yeah, definitely a demon," I say. "I've got this."

Do I piss myself just a little as I speak these words? Let's just say I can imagine it happening to someone else. It definitely doesn't help when the demon opens its mouth and acid drips out to burn a hole in the road. Great, there's that tar smell again. If the demon doesn't rip our heads off, we'll all die from lung disease. Wait, I'm the only one here technically alive. This does not make me feel better.

At least there's one thing working to my advantage. I've been on a low boil all night. While encountering a demon would normally set me off anyway, I just went from DEFCON 5 to DEFCON 1 in a matter of seconds.

Behind me, I hear Stephanie say, "Holy shit. Look at that."

This time, I know she means me. I have one arm cocked back, the other flexed at the ready, both hands already cradling crackling spheres of energy.

The demon drops back to all fours, getting ready to charge, but that's as far as it gets before I unleash my magic. As soon as I unload, I reload without even having to think about it. More bursts of magic flare from my hands, in a rapid series of blinding strikes. I keep driving the monster back, only to have it keep struggling forward.

From what feels like a million miles away, I hear Eric say, "I don't think she's got this."

That's enough to push me over the edge. I am just so over being tested right now, after days of freaking out in ways I never imagined. I let out a roar unlike any that's ever escaped my lips, this time pushing out both hands held together palms open. A massive blast of light shoots forth, doing way more than driving the demon back. Yes, it stumbles backwards, but then it bursts into flame burning as bright as magnesium. It takes only a few more seconds for it to sizzle down to it's already fading supernatural core.

For a few moments, all I'm aware of is the beating of my own heart as it desperately tries to slow. Then I hear voices behind me.

"What just happened?"

"You know what just happened. It was a demon."

"I know it was a demon, but why did it attack us? It's not supposed to work that way!"

As I come back to my senses, I hear Nora say, "Look, I don't know, but I told you guys we can trust her."

"Whatever," Stephanie says. "That demon came after us because of her."

"She's right," Eric says. "I'm out of here."

"Ditto," John says. "I'm sorry, Nora."

With the demon no longer blocking their way, and no humans present to observe them, the three vampires depart so quickly that my eyes can barely track them. They're at the end of the block and then gone before I have a chance to process what just happened.

For a moment, I expect Nora to leave too. Instead, she starts walking and I do the same, although I'm not sure where we're going.

As we leave the street, and thankfully the smell of burning tar behind, I turn to Nora. "What was up with your friends?"

"You mean why were they uncomfortable being attacked by a giant demon?"

When she puts it that way, it does seem like a silly question. "Well, I did tell you guys I had it under control."

Nora chuckles. "Was it me, or did it seem a little touch and go there for a moment?"

I waggle my hand. "Maybe just for a moment."

Nora brings her gaze back to mine. "The thing is, we never should have been in danger to begin with. Demons don't attack vampires. Not even inside the Inversion."

That one piques my interest, as I remember what Beatrice said about vampires crossing into that realm. Just to verify, I ask, "So, you guys can go there?"

To me, that sounds like veil witch magic, so how the hell does that work?

"Technically, yes," Nora says. "Personally, I've never paid a visit, but portals exist for those so inclined."

I feel my eyes narrow involuntarily.

Nora reads my reaction accurately. "We have an accord with the demons. It's not like we can open the veil."

What's weird is that I can tell she intends to set me at ease. Not exactly what I expected from my natural enemy.

Still, because I'm snooty about my veil witch territory, I say. "Of course not." Then I add, "But why would you guys go there at all? It's kind of a hellhole. Just saying."

We continue walking, now across a footbridge leaving the canal area. I figured we were through with searching for Mason tonight, but maybe not. Vampires don't exactly get tired and we still have time before daybreak.

"Like I said, I've never been, but some vampires go to partake of the Shared Feast. They say it strengthens the bond between between vampires and demons." She shudders and adds, "Look, that's just what I heard. I have no idea if it's even true."

I'm pretty darned sure I just stumbled onto something not even Beatrice knows about. There's just no way she wouldn't have mentioned something called the Shared Feast. At the same time, I can tell Nora wants to change the subject. So, I figure I might as well try to round out some of my other vampire knowledge.

"Just curious," I say. "That girl we put into the cab. Your, um, victim." I stop just short of saying *dinner.* "She seemed to be enjoying the experience. Let's just say it wasn't exactly the reaction I expected. Is it always that way?"

I would have heard about that, right? The witch community can't be that clueless.

Nora shakes her head. "Definitely not. What they experience is up to us, depending on how we influence that person."

I'm pretty sure what she means, but I figure it can't hurt to double-check. "Influence?"

"That's what we call it. Mind control just sounds so creepy."

Right, because vampires aren't creepy. I limit my response to, "Yeah, it sort of does."

"The thing is, everyone approaches it their own way, particularly when it comes to feeding."

She tries to leave it at that, but I'm nosy. "Based on what?"

Nora shrugs. "I don't know. Based on whether you're an asshole, or if you're basically nice. Or whatever inclinations you may have had in the past. Everybody's different. You know, kind of like people."

Ouch. But, to be fair, I walked right into that one. I decide to give it a rest while I get my bearings. We've covered a few miles, at least. Naturally—or maybe unnaturally—Nora seems completely unfazed by the trek. On the other hand, my legs are tired from trying to keep up, and I'm too proud to ask her to slow down.

"Where are we going?"

"Byrd Park," Nora says. "Since it's not too far."

Is she joking? That has to be a few more miles. What, exactly, is too far for a vampire? "I take it we're still looking for Mason."

In other words, she's not just hungry again, right?

"I figure it's worth a look." Nora checks the sky and adds, "After that I better bail. By the way, can you walk a little faster?"

CHAPTER 7

By the time we finally enter the park, my legs are all but worn out. It also feels like I'm getting blisters. Great. I didn't really think about it earlier, and just put on my boots. But if I'm going to keep doing these vampire workouts, I'm going to need new sneakers. Or maybe I can tap into that Regina thing and fly alongside Nora on these little death marches.

Thankfully, we slow our pace now that we're here. I take advantage of that to catch my breath, trying to inhale as silently as possible.

"Doing okay? Nora asks.

"Doing fine," I say. "How about you?"

Nora laughs softly, but doesn't bother answering the question. I didn't fool her, obviously.

I look around the park, taking in what I can. It's not much. The full moon, high in the sky before, has continued sinking toward the horizon. Clouds have also moved in during the time that's passed. As Nora scans the landscape, maybe she'll see something I don't.

A few moments pass and then she sighs. "Shit. Where is everyone?"

Definitely another first. I've never been around someone complaining of a lack of vampires. At the same time, I'm disappointed. I realize it's only been one night, but it's one more that Autumn remains charged with a magical crime.

Still, I can't think of anything either. "Should we call it?"

Nora scans the park again, and then glances at the sky. "Let's give it a few more minutes. You never know."

She's right, you never do, and it seems that Nora and I are a little alike. We jump in fast, blind to the risks as we try to get things done. We also don't forget when someone crosses someone we love.

Nora points down the path and says, "There's a bench over there. I wouldn't mind sitting. Come on."

I know she's doing it for me, but I take her up on the offer. We walk to the bench and sit beside each other.

"So…" I say.

Nora laughs softly. "You're not comfortable with silence, are you?"

She's right, obviously. On top of which, I'm nervously jiggling my knee. "You have no idea," I say.

She raises her eyebrows. "A veil witch thing?"

"For this veil witch, yes. I lost the ability to speak for a while. With my own voice." To clarify, I add, "I kind of lost my body too."

Nora whips around to look at me. "You're *that* veil witch?"

I shake my head, confused. "There's not very many of us." Shit, should I tell her that? It sounds like she didn't know. Trying to cover, I add, "I mean, there's enough."

"Dude," Nora says, "we know there's only two of you. Well, three now, apparently. But I wasn't sure if that was you or your sister."

Right, of course. I'm such an idiot. "Oh. Yeah, that was me."

"I hate those bastards," Nora says.

I know who she means, of course. The Vamanec P'yrin. Ironic. In the time that's passed, I've kept hating the vampires, while some of the Vamanec P'yrin—the same supernatural tribe I would have once exterminated without question—have become my friends. Well, Autumn's friends, mostly, but I know I can trust them.

"What about Ellis?" I say.

"Right, Ellis. I guess he's different. He must be if he works with the Shadow Order."

Which makes me wonder. "Have you ever run into any others?"

Nora shakes her head. "Not so far. Let's just say I've made a conscious effort over the years."

I can't blame her, of course, since the enmity between the Vamanec P'yrin and vampires goes back forever. It's strange to think, that for all the differences between those in the supernatural world and those who aren't part of it, in this way we're the same. Like our non-magical counterparts, we find reasons to hate those who are different.

I know I've already been more than my share of nosy for tonight, but I'm curious. "How many years?"

"A hundred and forty-seven," Nora says. "But who's counting, right?"

It shouldn't come as a surprise, but it still does. I guess because she looks so young.

"Did you, um, grow up here?" I'm not quite sure how to phrase it since she never quite finished growing up.

After a moment, Nora says, "Charleston. So, not too far, but it might as well have been a million miles back then."

The sadness in her voice tells me I shouldn't have asked. Which, now that I think about it, should have been obvious. I can't imagine there being a whole lot of happy vampire stories. So, I keep my response neutral. "I've never been to Charleston. I heard it's nice."

My guess is that we'll move on from there, but Nora says. "It was nice back then. Totally different, of course. A little seaport city, basically. Still kind of poor after the Civil War, but starting to bounce back. Honestly, I didn't think much about the war or any of that growing up. I guess because my family had money."

Since she's willing to talk about it, I say, "Did you have brothers and sisters?"

Nora shakes her head. "No, it was just me. Which I think made things worse. Maybe if I wasn't the only child…"

Her voice trails off, and I'm not sure what to say. I look out over the park, where the moon keeps sinking toward the horizon.

Nora sighs. "So, my father was sort of a big deal. He was the co-owner of one of the shipping companies. My mother was pretty much your typical southern belle. Very into fashion, parties, all that. Which was fine with me, until they decided it was time for me to get married. I was nineteen."

"Seems a little young."

"I felt the same way, but it really wasn't back then. So, I guess I should have expected it. Regardless, it still seemed like it fell out of the sky. Denial, I guess."

"Sure," I say. "You were just a kid."

A moment passes and Nora says. "Basically, but it wasn't just that. And it wasn't really even the guy they wanted me to marry. He was okay."

I glance over at her again. "You just didn't have feelings for him?"

Nora's eyes meet mine. She shrugs. "Well, that and I didn't really like boys."

"Oh."

Nora nods. "Right, oh. But I couldn't admit that, obviously. I barely understood it myself. I thought something had to be wrong with me. But I refused to get married. Things got bad. Then they got worse. And one day I just ran away."

I figure we're in this deep already, so there's no point in pretending otherwise. "So, is that when you came here?"

"No, that was still a ways off. I ended up in Charlotte for a while, where I managed to find work as a nanny. But there were problems with that too, since I caught the eye of my mistress's husband. She decided I might be a little less attractive if I had a few bruises on my face. So, obviously, that didn't work out. From there, I wandered up to Raleigh. Only, this time I didn't find work at all. At that point, I was dirty, scared and half-starved. I knew I'd made a mistake, and I figured it was time to head home again. Only, I was out of money and had no prospects. So, like many a desperate girl before me..."

Nora lets her words trail off again, but her meaning is clear. Before I utter a useless response, she continues.

"It was called the Brick House Tavern. Pretty much what you'd think. A saloon mostly, some food if anyone wanted it. Pool and poker. A real gentleman's club. And, of course, there were women. Well, girls, really. Of course, that's where the real money was being made." She pauses. "But look, that was a million years ago. And, well, obviously I was a different person. Besides, pretty soon I met Claire and everything changed."

Nora puts just enough emphasis on the word "everything" that I suspect what she means. To be on the safe side, I just say, "Who was Claire?"

Nora's voice brightens. "Well, one night I decided to take a walk in a park quite a bit like this one. I planned on it being my last night in Raleigh. I figured I had enough money squirreled away to make it back home. Anyway, I was strolling under the stars when I met a very interesting lady. Just a little older than me. Very well dressed, mysterious, and undeniably attractive. Well, let's just say that she liked me, I liked her, and one thing led to another. I didn't leave Raleigh the next day, and I never returned to Charleston."

So, I was right. When she said "everything," she meant *that* "everything." But it also means I was wrong about something else. "So, I guess you weren't turned against your will."

Nora shakes her head. "Right. I knew what Claire was. Or, at least, as best as I could understand it. But it didn't matter. For me to be with her, *truly* be with her, something had to change. Just for the record, I know how often it goes the other way—more often than not, as you probably suspect—but she didn't force it on me. She never even pressured me. I made the choice."

I know there are those who choose to be vampires, but I've always imagined it differently. Something resulting from a lust for immortality, the desire to be powerful, or an attraction to the darker side of our nature. It never occurred to me that it could result from love. At the same time, Nora hasn't mentioned Claire being one of those who perished last night.

I hesitate, but then say, "Something happened to Claire, didn't it?"

Nora nods. "Yes, about thirty years after we met. Somehow the hunters found out about her. They killed her. Veil witches aren't the only ones who kill vampires. They're just the only ones who use magic."

Her words sting, but there's no accusation in her voice. Like before, she's just stating the facts. The way things are. I guess when you've lived as long as she has, it's easier to accept.

I'm about to ask how those vampire hunters didn't find her, and how she ended up living here, but suddenly she perches forward.

"We need to move. Right now." Nora jumps up, about to run off, but then turns back. "Come on!"

I jump to my feet, following Nora as she starts running back to where we entered the park. "What the hell is it?" I look through the darkness, still seeing nothing.

Nora is getting ahead of me, gaining distance fast. I guess she can't help it. Then she stops. She stands stock still, sniffing the air.

"Oh, shit," she says. "It's too late."

Then I look past her and see glowing amber eyes staring back at us. At first, I think they're demons. Then they draw forward, their shadowy forms becoming more defined. Wolves. Only they're massive, nearly the size of lions. Collectively, they growl, softly at first, but those growls keep growing louder.

This can't be happening. This seriously can't be happening.

I suddenly remember something that barely registered before. The full moon! Veil witches aren't the primary predator of the vampires. Not by a long shot. There might be a truce going on, but apparently tonight that doesn't matter. Because the true predator of vampires has always been werewolves, and these werewolves seem very much focused on Nora.

There's four of them, fanned out in a semi-circle and drawing closer. I check behind us to make sure there aren't more penning us in. I don't see any, so that's good. But that's the only good news, and we're still outnumbered two to one. The wolves keep drawing forward, their muzzles pulled back and their teeth dripping saliva.

I whisper to Nora. "What do we do?"

"How the hell would I know?"

Great, she's lived for over a hundred years and she's never faced off against a werewolf before? Oh, right. If she had, she probably wouldn't be here. The problem being I've never faced off against one either. The only time I've even seen one was when Autumn's pal, Dylan, showed up in wolf form to protect her. Desperate, I latch onto that angle.

I try my most soothing voice. "Hey, are any of you guys named Dylan?"

My question is met with more growling, as the werewolves gain more ground and we keep stepping back. Fangs, already exposed, become even more so. I try not to imagine my flesh being ripped from my bones.

Just in case they didn't hear me, I try again. "Seriously, guys. Dylan and I are buds. We had dinner together a few weeks ago. Well, technically, it was my sister's boyfriend's birthday, so there was a group of us, but—"

The growling grows in intensity, to the point where my primal fear is nearly paralyzing. Apparently, my rambling is getting on the werewolves' nerves. Fair enough. I was kind of annoying myself.

I look at Nora side-eyed. "Show them your fangs."

"Fuck off. Show them yours."

Okay, not quite the response I expected, but it was a lame idea. We could turn and run, but then we'd expose our backs. Besides, I'm not sure even Nora can outrun a werewolf. Opening the veil won't do the trick since, unlike vampires, werewolves are natural to our realm.

Come on, come on, come on! Think of something!

In a few seconds that feel like a lifetime, my brain keeps spinning and getting nowhere. Then I realize I'm thinking in the wrong direction. Don't think supernatural, think earth. Think primal fear. Animals. Fire. Yes!

I summon magic once more, praying I'm not out of juice from the last battle. I thrust out both hands, the fear within me flaring into orbs of supernova intensity. In an instant, the sky above washes out and my own sight dims as Nora yelps in pain. Shit, that's right. This much light must be excruciating to her, but I can't worry about that now.

I shift my focus back to the wolves. They're hunkered down, digging their oversized paws into the earth. They keep their heads lowered and their ears flat against their skulls. Their teeth, however, remain very much bared. Damn. What does it take to make these guys back off? I mean, come on, I'm bringing a vampire to her knees.

As if in response, the alpha out front launches himself into the air. I have a split second to shift my focus away from the pack to its now airborne leader. I act instinctively, hurling one of the crackling energy spheres. It collapses in on itself, streaking through the air like a missile. The werewolf lets out a squeal of pain and flies backwards, where it plunges to the ground and slides through the grass. The rest of the pack halts, their eyes locked warily on me.

I screw up my courage and take an aggressive step toward them, my message being, *You want to know who's the real alpha here, bitches? Just take a look at your fallen comrade.*

Only, their fallen comrade doesn't stay fallen. He climbs back to his feet and starts advancing again. How the hell is that even possible?

I can only guess that the kind of magic that would totally smoke a full-on supernatural being only serves to discourage a werewolf. Unlike vampires and demons, werewolves are supernatural hybrids. They're magically enhanced combinations of natural elements. Man and wolf combined, a freakish fusion, but still one originating in this dimension.

How the hell are we supposed to fight them? More importantly, why didn't I look into it before now? Idiot. Those old movies come to mind, where they use silver bullets, but I don't have any of those. Or a gun to shoot them with. By the look of things, I have about two seconds before all four werewolves leap this time. Great, after everything, I'm going out as dog food.

But then the image of airborne werewolves connects me with another image—that of myself recently deflecting an incoming barrage of rocks. I wasn't wrong about the werewolves, who collectively leap into the air, their milky fangs rocketing toward my jugular from four directions. I thrust out the arms I'd pulled in to protect myself. This time the objective isn't to ignite flares of light, but rather to exert as much deflection force as magically possible. As a group, the wolves suddenly rocket backwards. And I must not have been messing around, because the four-legged dickheads keep toppling end over end until they're clean out of sight. In the dark, it's hard to be sure how far they travel, but by the time thuds reach my ears, accompanied by yelps of pain, I'm pretty sure I nearly hit them out of the park.

I turn to Nora and shout, "Run!"

Apparently, she's more than happy to oblige since, within moments, I can't see her anymore either.

CHAPTER 8

I'm still running full-bore when, half a mile past the park, something latches onto my arm and jerks me to a stop. Of course, only someone with supernatural strength could make that happen. I literally lurch from top speed to a complete standstill in an instant. Damn, my arm is going to be sore tomorrow.

Nora stares back at me, her pale blue eyes now the ones glowing in the darkness. "They're gone," she says. "We're okay."

I realize that she's right, of course. I've been tearing through the streets like a woman on fire for no reason. The werewolves never left the park. Maybe flying through the air mixed them up too much. Or, even better, scared the hell out of them. Maybe they lost our scent. Either way, we're safe.

Now that I can finally think, I can't help but wonder what drew them to that park to begin with. The werewolves in this territory don't hunt humans, but they do hunt vampires. Well, they did before the truce, but they couldn't have possibly known we were coming. I also got the feeling they were pretty damned tweaked out before we arrived. I kind of doubt that was just because of the full moon. More like they'd been compelled into hunting mode by something they'd found impossible to resist. Then we came along as a potential appetizer before the main course.

Nora seems otherwise preoccupied. Understandably, because while it's still dark it won't be for long.

I bend over to suck in a few more deep breaths, and then straighten up again. "Time to get home, I guess." Then something occurs to me. "Where are you staying?"

It hasn't come up, but I assume she can't return to where she's been living. At least, not until it's safe.

Nora shakes her head. "Not sure. I meant to ask Steph and those guys but then that demon thing happened?"

Then we just went to a park and you forgot all about it? I don't say that, of course, and I suppose she might be in denial. After all, last night her vampire family was still alive. Come to think of it, I know nothing about them, but this definitely isn't the time. And clearly she didn't arrange for another night of Shadow Order protection. Why, I have no idea, but we can't worry about that now either.

Nora keeps watching me, no doubt waiting for me to say something. Seriously? She can't be thinking that, can she? She must just be messing with me again. So I say, "How about my place?"

She smiles her little vampire smile and says. "Really? Are you sure you don't mind?"

~~~

Since the Cauldron isn't too far off—and because Nora keeps me moving like a bat out of hell—we arrive with time to spare. Thankfully, for once there's no party going on, so I don't have to face the door troll, after facing off against werewolves, after facing off against a demon. Things appear to be looking up.

As we climb the stairs, Nora says, "What's with the flying frog?"

"Don't ask," I say. Fucking snorflers. Apparently, once you have them, you're stuck with them.

I unlock my door, step inside and turn back to Nora. I gesture in a sweeping motion. "Would you like to come in?"

Nora stares at me flatly. "Really?"

My face grows warm. "I heard it was a thing. That you had to be, you know, invited in."

"I'm a vampire, not a leprechaun," Nora says, as she enters the apartment. "Man, the stuff people come up with." She looks around and adds, "Nice place. This is the witch hangout, right?"

She doesn't seem nervous, but I guess there's no reason she should be. While vampires and witches have a rocky history, I'm the only resident veil witch.

"We call it the Cauldron," I say.

Nora flops down on the sofa. "A little on the nose, don't you think? But, yeah, we all know about this place. It has a reputation for parties."

I'm not sure if our blocking charms work on vampires, or if those are just magically calibrated for humans. My guess is humans, since presumably most of our neighbors fall into that category. And it's not like we'd be keeping any nearby vampires awake.

"There's definitely a social aspect," I admit. "By the way, please promise you won't consume anyone living in the building."

Nora raises an eyebrow. "Consume?"

"I don't know," I say, as I walk toward the kitchen. "What do you call it?"

"We just call it feeding. It's not like we swallow them."

I shrug and open the fridge. "Want a—? Never mind." I get myself a beer, pop it open and go back into the living room. "You wouldn't, right?"

Nora holds up three fingers. "Scout's honor. Besides, witch blood tastes weird."

I have no idea how to react. Strangely, I'm mildly insulted. "Weird how?"

Nora shrugs. "Just sort of, you know, too strong."

No, I don't know, and I'm hesitant to ask how she does. I've always heard the phrase "witch blood" and now it seems like there really is a difference. I take the loveseat. "So, is it the magic?"

Nora nods. "Definitely. It tastes like cayenne."

She shudders at the thought, so I guess that's comforting. Especially since she'll be staying the night. I mean day. This is going to be weird.

Nora's attention is suddenly caught by something across the room. She gestures with her head. "Wait, did you—?"

I follow her gaze to the mirror I hung by the front door. A little reminder, for all those times I forget to brush my hair. Presently, it has a towel draped over it. It takes me a moment, but I have to laugh.

"Nothing to do with you," I say. "But let me guess, that one isn't true either."

Nora shakes her head. "We can see ourselves in mirrors. Not that I'm worried about it. I've looked the same for over a century. By the way, the garlic thing is BS too. I've never been sure what that's about. Like we're afraid of getting heartburn or something. Then there's my all-time favorite, the seed legend. "

I shake my head, confused. "What's that about?"

Nora shrugs. "Right, that one's a little obscure. You don't hear it much anymore, but it was once believed that if you scattered seeds we'd have to stop and count them. I guess people back then thought we were all OCD or something."

"Safe to assume you guys can't change into bats?"

Nora laughs. "Right, that one too. Besides, who'd want to turn into a bat? Have you ever seen a bat's face?"

Again, I find myself laughing. Not exactly what I expected from hanging out with a vampire. Not that I ever expected to find myself hanging out with a vampire. The thing is, I can't help but like Nora. At the same time, I keep experiencing a mild buzzing feeling. I've managed to suppress it all night, but it's there all the same, a faint agitation reminding me that we're supposed to be enemies. Like a little voice saying, *Don't forget to kill her.*

I try not to think about it, but I've taken out more than a few vampires in the past. Which has always been pretty grim, considering they don't just get shoved through the veil. Vampire magic may not originate here, but those who've been turned did. So, striking them with veil witch magic separates the natural from the supernatural. The result being instant decomposition to either dust or a pile of bones, depending on when the vampire was turned. I suppose if you caught one soon enough you'd end up with a rotting corpse. Thankfully, I haven't had that experience.

I remind myself that those other vampire encounters were different, each time involving truly nasty characters. It had been a matter of survival. Maybe I'm just rationalizing, but I also felt sure that those I'd faced off against were killers. I'd just *felt* it.

Nora snaps me out. "What's up? You sort of checked out there for a minute."

I can't quite bring myself to tell her. Instead, I keep it to, "It's strange, the two of us sitting here like this. Me being a veil witch and all."

Nora thinks about that for a moment, like she almost forgot. "Oh, right. Pretty much your primary objective is to remove vermin like me."

I wasn't going to quite phrase it that way, but still. "Something like that."

"Yeah, well, maybe that can wait. I don't know about you, but I'm tired." Nora stretches and yawns. I can't help but notice that, even if they're retracted, she still has noticeably pointy canines. She looks around and says, "I don't imagine you have any rooms without windows."

My eyes flick back and forth, and then I shake my head. "Nothing like that."

Nora looks disappointed. "Not even the bathroom?"

"Sorry." I'm not really sorry, since I can't imagine going an entire day without using my bathroom.

Nora nods, as if resigned to her fate. "I guess it will have to be the closet. I hate closets. They smell funny and there's always spiders."

"I guess we could vacuum it," I say.

"That'd be great. And maybe a blanket and pillow too? I mean, if it's not a problem."

She yawns again and gets up from the sofa. I guess what goes for humans, goes for humans and vampires too, since her yawn makes me yawn. Then I get up off the loveseat. It's time to get the vampire ready for bed.

CHAPTER 9

I don't think I've ever showed up for work at Grimoire on time. Technically, my shift starts at ten (yes, I know, such a rigorous schedule), but last night left me beat. By the time I get my act together and stride through the door, it's pushing eleven. Hoping Maggie's not too mad, I say, "Good morning, Mags. Sorry I'm late."

I always say that, so it's not like I expect that alone to trigger a reaction. If anything, Maggie would probably notice if I didn't apologize when I showed up.

As usual, she's reading a book. And, as usual, she barely looks up. "No worries, sweetie. I made coffee cake if you're interested. Tea's out back too. Hope you're okay with Earl Grey. I ran out of English Breakfast."

Seriously, coffee cake? Damn, I can't remember the last time I had coffee cake. I try to keep from licking my lips as I think about sweet buttery cinnamon and brown sugar crumble. I guess I'll just have to deal with the inconvenience of washing it down with Earl Grey.

I snag a slice of coffee cake, fill a mug of tea, and pop back out front. I settle onto one of barstools we keep behind the counter. And there we are, two witches managing the register in an empty magical bookstore.

Maggie looks up from her reading. "Just so you know, I added new wards both inside and outside."

I look at her, my cheeks bulging with coffee cake. Like everything Maggie bakes, it's incredibly good. I nod, making the connection. Of course she means the speculomancy thing. That couldn't possibly have been a coincidence.

"Good idea," I say. In truth, I suspect our rogue veil witch has moved on from that magical method. It's just too imprecise to be anything more than some sort of weird calling card.

Maggie takes a sip of her tea, looking me up and down. "Isn't it a little cold for shorts?"

I swallow another bite of coffee cake. "I was thinking about going for a run."

Maggie's brow furrows. "When did you start running?"

A fair question, given that I've never mentioned running before. Because I've never been running before. Not if I wasn't being chased. I'm wearing shorts because a vampire is sleeping in my closet. I found them in my lowest bathroom drawer. How they got there, I have no idea. Thankfully, I left a semi-clean sweatshirt on my couch, where I also slept, since sleeping in the bedroom just seemed weird

"As it turns out, I didn't," I say. "Maybe tomorrow."

Maggie chuckles. "Don't I know it. I joined a gym three years ago and I've probably been three times." She sighs and adds, "I really should cancel that membership."

For the life of me, I can't imagine Maggie hitting the gym. Besides, given the number of men in her life, I just figured she was on the frequent sex fitness plan.

For a few moments, we sit in silence while Maggie sips her tea and I scarf down my coffee cake. When I look at Maggie again, I see that her expression has shifted to one of concern.

She speaks softly. "How's your sister doing?"

Of course she knows about what happened. Word of someone having their powers bound must travel like wildfire. Losing her magic is every witch's greatest fear. "She's okay," I say. "Autumn is strong. She'll get through this. *We'll* get through this."

Maggie touches the back of my hand. "I feel just terrible about it. I'm so sorry."

For a moment, I think she means it in a general sense, but then I look into her eyes again. "What? No! Maggie, it's not your fault!"

She frowns. "Well, it is partly, isn't it? I should have kept my mouth shut at that stupid coven meeting. But no. I fell right into it, didn't I? Sarah Wellingsford asked me what I thought and I had to just go and say that speculomancy was associated with veil witches. I should have just lied. Besides, who knows, really? No one uses that kind of magic anymore. Why would they?"

Exactly, why would they? To let you know you're being watched. To throw you off your game. To rattle you, to scare you, to let you know you aren't unique in your powers anymore. To name a few reasons, but which one is it? And for what purpose in the long run? What game are we playing and just how many players are there?

But none of that matters now, as Maggie's face turns red with emotion and her eyes glisten with regret, her words reminding me again that I have some very good friends in the witch community.

"Sarah Wellingsford set you up," I say. "She used you."

"Why would she do that?"

"I don't know. Not yet, but I'm working on it." I bring my eyes to hers again. "What do you know about her?"

Maggie thinks for a moment as she sips her tea. "Well, she has a long history as a powerful witch. She's very much part of the community but, at the same time, tends to keep her distance. I guess she's private, overall. That's not unusual in and of itself."

Something in Maggie's tone makes me perch forward. "But?"

"Well, my understanding is that there was a time when she remained less reclusive. Before her husband died, but that was a long time ago."

"How long?"

Maggie glances at the ceiling. "Thirty years, give or take? They say his death hit her hard, that she grieved for a long time. It was nearly a decade before she surfaced."

A decade? Sure, loss is a bitch, but humans move on a different timeline. Even for a witch, a decade seems long. The back of my neck tingles and there's no way I'm ignoring it.

"What do you know about her husband?"

"Not very much. Only that he was also reputed to be a powerful witch. Like Sarah, from a pure blood family. And of course that his death was mysterious."

Well, look at that. My neck tingling just increased a little more. "Mysterious how?"

"Well, violent, for one thing. They found him in the woods a few miles from the Wellingsford's estate. They say he was nearly torn apart."

I cock an eyebrow at that one. "Werewolves?"

Maggie shrugs. "It was never determined. Some said werewolves, others vampires. And there were those who thought it might be the work of demons, carried out at Sarah's command. That possibly she'd been dabbling in dark magic. I was young at the time, but my mother said that was just gossip. Apparently, there'd been talk of some strain in the Wellingsford's marriage. Which, of course, led to tongues wagging. That sort of thing is always going to happen when there's a violent, unsolved death."

"So, they never found out," I say.

Maggie sips her tea. "They never did."

Sounds about right, for some reason. From what I've seen of Sarah, I bet she did it with her bare hands. The guy probably left the seat up or something. My blood starts to boil as Sarah Wellingsford's face looms inside my mind. I take a deep silent breath, willing myself to calm down. It's not going to do me or Maggie any good if I get myself worked up. For all I know, I might inadvertently summon my magic and blow a hole in the side of Maggie's bookstore.

At least burrowing into Sarah Wellingsford's shady past has one good effect. It appears that Maggie has, at least for the moment, stopped blaming herself. Before she shifts back into that mode, I decide to go in a different direction.

"Before I forget, do we have anything out back about creating a battery?"

Maggie knows what I mean, of course. It takes her less than three seconds. "Five books, I believe. Oh, wait. Make that four. I have two copies of P.J. Duckworth's 'Complete Guide to Transference for Beginners.' Have you read that yet?"

Um, no. But I've been meaning to get to it? I just shake my head.

"That's probably a great place to start. What were you planning to use as your talisman?"

I reach into my pocket and withdraw a smooth blue oblong stone. I hold it out in my palm for Maggie to see.

"Isn't that lovely," she says. "I'm sure it will hold magic nicely. It has an almost unearthly luster, doesn't it? Wherever did you get it?"

"I found it in the forest."

Not an outright lie, but Maggie guessed right about the unearthly luster. I picked up the stone one morning while out walking with Esras. This was after the fall of the Seelie regime, when there had finally been time for leisurely strolls. Before that, we would have been running or hiding.

I start to get off my stool but Maggie stops me. "I know exactly where they are," she says. "You just stay right there and enjoy your breakfast."

I should argue with that, but Maggie really will find the books more quickly. The indexing system at Grimoire is fairly insane, with books being arranged according to magical association. So, books about abjuration magic are grouped with those about thaumaturgy, since the magical principles regarding protection and healing hold much in common. Same goes for blood magic and elemental magic, despite one often being associated with dark arts and the other carrying almost entirely positive connotations. The connection there being that both involve harnessing natural energy sources. I've worked at Grimoire for two months and I'm still getting it down.

I'm just about done with my coffee cake when Maggie returns with the books. "These should do the trick," she says. Have you ever attempted transference before?"

"Is it difficult?" To judge by Maggie's expression, I get the feeling it might be.

She shrugs. "Like any spell, it can involve a bit of learning. In some ways, it's similar to creating charms or wards, since both involve imbuing an object with magic. But that's not quite the same as getting an object to store magic. Come to think of it, I've never tried. I'll be interested to see how it goes."

Maggie's eyes meet mine, and I can tell she knows what I'm up to. Trying to give Autumn access to some of my magic. I have no idea if it can work against a binding, but I figure it's worth a try.

Maggie checks her phone to read a text. Since I'm here, she must have a date. That's the way it usually goes. Still, she says, "Would you like me to make more tea? It's such a chilly day."

I hold up my mostly still full mug. "Nope. I'm good. I can always make more."

Maggie gestures to the books. "Do you need any help with those? They can make for some pretty dense reading, especially with—"

"Maggie, go," I say. "Tom's probably waiting for you." I'm just taking a stab at it, since last time she was having lunch with Tom. Honestly, I think *having lunch* is just a euphemism for getting in a workout. There's no way Maggie is hungry after chowing down with me every morning. At least not for food.

Maggie blushes a little. "Actually, today I'm meeting with Adam. He's such a sweetie. Have you met him?"

"Um, maybe?" The fact is, it's hard to keep track. Maggie must have some sort of magical pheromone for attracting men her age, as well as some quite a bit younger.

Maggie winks and laughs. "Oh, if you met Adam, you'd remember. Believe me."

I have to laugh too, and I do believe her. Maggie may be pushing sixty, but she doesn't mess around when it comes to men. Or maybe it's just that she has a way of keeping them in really good shape.

"Don't worry. I'll hold down the fort," I say. "Go on out there and show them what you're made of."

Maybe not the best choice of phrasing, since Maggie's face turns red. But that doesn't keep her from putting her coat on and bustling out the door. Maggie Greene:

elemental witch, bibliophile, baker extraordinaire and sex goddess. I have no doubt that her Book of Shadows will make for truly educational reading for whoever is lucky enough to get her hands on it someday.

CHAPTER 10

With Maggie gone, I have hours to kill in a bookstore likely to remain empty for most of the day. Not that I'm complaining. A warm cozy spot to sip tea, munch on coffee cake (yes, I go for round two on that deal) and pore over books of magic seems like a little slice of heaven. Especially after last night's slice of hell.

Just to be sure, I glance at the window before taking the blue Faerie stone back out of my pocket. Seeing that the coast is clear, I open one of the books Maggie brought to me. I'm about to go for it when the door opens. An old guy walks in talking on his phone. After meeting Grayson at Grimoire, magically cloaked to look like a nursing home resident, naturally my guard goes up.

"What the heck is a karmic contract?" the guys says into his phone. "Didn't you already read that one?" A beat and then he sighs. "Oh, that was the one about soul connections. Not sure how I could mix those up. Okay, I'll look."

Yeah, definitely not a fae mage masked to look human. More like disgruntled husband sent shopping. I slip the stone back into my pocket and close the book. There's no point anyway right now.

The old guy listens for a few more seconds. "Seriously? What do we need sage for?" Another beat and then, "What the hell is a hell sky?"

I have to look up at that one.

"Is that what they're calling it now? Okay, sure, I heard about the birds. What was it this time? Come on, Phyllis, you really have to stop paying attention to all of this non—"

Apparently, Phyllis isn't having it since the guy falls silent as he listens. Only this time, I'm listening too while pulling the news up on my phone.

"What, trees this time? Wasn't it trees the first time? Okay, so sue me. That was crops. Dead crops, dead birds, dead trees. Probably some sort of blight."

Okay, there it is, I found it. It's not on any of the big news carriers, but one of the local news websites reports that, last night, people observed the sky turning bright red. Apparently, come morning, all of the trees in that part of town were found twisted and blackened.

"What do you mean, a demon? Oh, come on!"

I keep scrolling and find a link to a related story. *Neighbors report seeing unidentified creature.* A chill ripples down my spine. Yep, that has to be it. I click on the link to read that, last night, there were several reports to the police department from people claiming to see some sort of creature running through the streets. Some reported seeing a man, while others described it as a large animal, possibly a bull. Apparently all claimed it had horns. Damn, sounds familiar.

I can't help but wonder if it might have been the same demon I faced off against. But how could people see it? I thought demons could only be seen by other supernatural creatures, and not many at that. Has something shifted with the veil, allowing through demons with more power to manifest in this realm physically? I just don't know, but this isn't good.

I look up as the old guy approaches the counter.

"Do you have a book about something called a comic contract?"

Seriously, he forgot already? "Karmic Contracts," I say. "It's over there in the Reincarnation section." I only know this because it's one of the new ones that's been selling well. A bit of a rage in woo-woo circles.

The guy wanders off, finds the endcap display, and wanders back again, book in hand.

"This it?" I nod and he adds, "Seriously, twenty dollars?"

Poor Phyllis.

"Yes, but it comes with free sage," I say, holding up a packet of the stuff. This isn't true normally, but I'm trying to move things along. My ploy seems to work, since the guy digs out his wallet. I ring him up and he finally leaves.

Now, back to my project, although I have to admit that the interruption was educational. Hell Sky? The thing has a name now?

I flip open the transference magic book again and set my Faerie stone back out on the counter. An hour passes, and then another as I keep trying the spells. Then, finally, I remember something that might be interfering. In fact, when it finally dawns on me, it seems obvious. If I'm hiding part of myself, how can I transfer part of myself to the talisman. As weird as that seems, that's what I'm doing, right?

Okay, it's time to lower the glamour, which I probably shouldn't do right now. Then again, I already had my customer for the day. I let my ears out and try the spell again. This time, my blue Faerie stone starts to tremble. Then it starts to glow, becoming enveloped in golden light, as tiny arcs of electricity shoot from my fingertips.

My head snaps up as three women walk past the front window, probably heading to one of the nearby boutiques. Not that there's necessarily a typical Grimoire customer, but they look a little too well packaged. It turns out I'm wrong, since a moment later three affluent looking suburban mom types walk in as I scramble to glamour my elf ears.

"Seriously, you've never been in here?" one of them says. "This place is a riot."

She's thin, tall and blonde alongside her two brunette friends.

"Oh, wow, check this out," a brunette says. She stands, hands on hips as she scans the signs marking the sections. "Angels and spirit guides, tarot and oracle, astrology, divination and numerology. You weren't kidding!"

"I know, it's nuts," the other brunette says. "Can you imagine the people who actually shop here? What a bunch of gullible dipshits."

The blonde snorts out a laugh. "Come here and check out these fliers. They're just ridiculous."

They cluster at the bulletin board and start tittering. So far, my presence hasn't been acknowledged, so I guess they just don't care if I hear things like, "What the hell is a psychic fair? Do you get to, like, ride a psychic?" or "Crystal and vibrational healing. I know which one I'm going for," but then they cross the line.

"Hey, check this one out. Some fool is advertising a supernatural cleaning service. Let me guess, she uses magic to lift stains from your carpet." This comes from the blonde, obviously the ringleader. A brunette chimes in next. "Wait, maybe she shampoos your ghosts." Apparently they find that hilarious, since it elicits another round of tittering, followed by Brunette Number Two saying, "God, too funny. What a load of crap."

Okay, that's it. I have things to do and these three must be late for their manicure. I clear my throat loud enough that they finally look my way. All three of them gasp and go wide-eyed. And, no, I'm not worried about them telling anyone later about what they saw. Who's going to believe some story about a pointy-eared girl shooting electricity from her fingertips toward a glowing blue stone? Especially one who, as she continues to stare back, levitates into the air. As they scramble out the door, I'm pretty sure they'll soon know what it's like to be called a gullible dipshit.

I give a friendly wave as they dart past the window, and then lower myself back onto my stool. Thanks, Regina, for the inspiration. I can now say I've successfully flown. Well, okay, hovered, but it's a start.

~~~

Once I get my concentration back into gear, it takes almost a full hour of zapping away at my Faerie stone before it stops becoming wrapped in golden light. After that, my fingers start to burn. I double-check the magic book and, sure enough, that means you've created your talisman. Also, according to the book, you've most likely stored a significant magical boost, but it might not last long. An hour, tops, depending on how much you use. To transfer more, you need to repeat the procedure on a daily basis for at least a week. Damn, I guess I should have read through the chapter first. Still, an hour is better than nothing.

I heave out a sigh and get to my feet, slipping the stone back into my pocket. I go to the window and stare out at the street. The sidewalks are empty and the sky clouding over like it might rain. When before I felt cozy and comforted, I begin to feel edgy. Out there another day is passing, which means we're another day closer to Autumn's trial. We're down to four days, and am I any closer to having answers? Maybe a little, but not nearly enough. Tears suddenly prick at my eyes, a feeling of helplessness welling within me.

And then there's Bethany, isn't there? The coven meeting was now two nights ago, which means she's been gone... what? A week? More? How long until her image fades from that mirror? My feeling of helplessness continues to build, and with it my anger. Magic rises within me, bubbling its way to the surface. All I want to do is lash out. I want to blow apart bookshelves and smash out windows. I want to kill and destroy, when I can't even find my enemy.

I spin away from the window so no one can see me. I pull my hair back and yell, "Shit!" Then I start to pace back and forth across the floor. I could swear I actually hear the seconds ticking past, as together they build to swallow time.

Four days... four days... four days...

~~~

By the time Maggie returns, I've managed to compose myself again. The last thing she needs is me adding to her guilt by flipping out in front of her. She bustles in, her cheeks red from the cold. She peels off her jacket, as always offering a smile.

"I hope I wasn't too long," she says.

The fact is, she's back sooner than normal. Usually, she comes back closer to closing time.

"No worries," I say. "Everything's fine. And, hey, we made a sale."

Maggie hangs her coat on her hook. "Let me guess, Karmic Contract."

I have to laugh. "Bingo. How'd you guess?"

"Well, it's not hurting anyone," Maggie says. "And there's truth in there too. We really do have to balance the scales eventually."

I get up off my stool, gathering up the magic books I used earlier. I look at Maggie and raise an eyebrow. "Let me guess... Alchemy?"

Maggie chuckles. "A good guess, and a logical one."

"But... no," I say.

"I'm afraid not, dear. Alchemy is transforming objects. Transference magic is—"

"Weaponry magic?"

"No."

"Earth magic?"

"Um, no."

"Projection magic."

Maggie shrugs. "*Close...*"

"Absorption magic?"

Maggie reaches for the book. "It's fine, dear. Why don't I just—"

"Chi magic!"

Maggie raises her eyebrows. "Very *good*," she says. "That's it, precisely, because in order to shift your power to another vessel, you first have to reach into your core. See, you're getting it!"

Right, give me another ten years and I should be fine. All the same, as I take the books out back to the Special Collections room, I feel a little proud of myself. Maybe I shouldn't—it took me like ten tries—but I felt pretty sure about that chi magic thing when I finally got there. I find that section and slide the books back into their places.

I'm about to leave the room when my eyes drift to the shelf I've gone to most often lately. It's almost involuntary now, checking that spot where Lauren Flannery's Book of Shadows sits alongside the others. Part of me has kept meaning to take it home, while another part of me has remained hesitant. I guess because the connection was just too unnerving.

I suddenly realize it's gone. I do a double-take, and then walk closer just to be sure. I stare at the gaping spot where now one book leans to rest against another. I try telling myself I should feel relieved. That I should take it to mean that Lauren's book—with its heartbreaking account of betrayal—no longer has a place in my life. Instead, an icy chill travels through me. Along with it comes a sense of foreboding.

I go back out front, feeling numb and trying not to show my shock. Maybe it's a mistake. Someone probably just looked through the book and failed to put it back again.

"Everything okay?" Maggie says. "You look a little… ruffled."

I try to smile. "Sure, I'm fine. It's just… Do you remember that Book of Shadows? The one that seemed like it reached out to me?"

Maggie knows that part, since we talked about how it just somehow appeared on the counter one morning, as if waiting for me. I just didn't burden her with the rest. "Yes, of course," she says. "Lauren Flannery's book."

"Where did it go?"

"Well, that was the strangest thing," Maggie says. "I meant to tell you. A young witch came in and bought it."

I feel like I'm looking at Maggie through a tunnel, the world closing in around me. "A young witch. Who was it?"

Maggie shakes her head. "I'd never seen him before, but he seemed nice."

"Him, you said."

"Yes, him. Rather an interesting looking young man, with hair that was almost white. He had the most striking blue eyes. You'll never guess what he said."

That chill keeps spreading within me. "What's that?"

"He said he'd been traveling, and that's where he heard about our store. Turns out he met someone we both know."

I overcome my numbness long enough to utter one word. "Grayson."

"Yes, Grayson! So, I guess that solves that mystery of where Grayson disappeared to. He must have gone traveling again."

CHAPTER 11

With nightfall still a few hours off, I assume that Nora is still snoozing away in my closet. Come to think of it, I really don't know much about how vampires sleep either, except what I've seen in movies. In those, the vampire basically turns into a statue—pale, stiff and laying on its back. But what's the reality? Do some curl up and sleep on their side? Do they snore? Fart? Probably not, right? Vampires would have been hunted down and wiped out long ago if you could hear them snoring and farting.

And what about that other part? Nora said her lover, Claire, was killed by hunters. How does that work? For me, snuffing out vampires is a snap. I just light up an orb, send it flying and then, poof, dust and bones. But what about my non-magical counterparts? Is it true that they resort to hammers and wooden stakes? I guess I should ask Nora. Would that be insensitive? I guess maybe a little.

These are my thoughts as I stroll the sidewalk on Franklin Street heading toward the VCU campus. I'm not sure what my odds are, but I know Autumn has a class ending at five. Some sort of workshop in the Fine Arts Building. She's mentioned it a few times, since that class is one of her favorites, except apparently that building is always cold. If nothing else, I'm a good listener.

I arrive just as people start to spill out. These are older, grad school types, so it looks like I timed things right. A moment later, Autumn comes down the steps. She walks by without seeing me, but it's not like I told her I was coming. I follow after her just as a breeze blows back her hair. Oh, no. Does she know her ears are showing?

I trot up beside her and tap her on the shoulder. "Hey, buddy. How's it going?"

Autumn breaks her stride, her face lighting up in a smile. "What are you doing here?"

"Just sort of in the neighborhood," I say.

Understandably, Autumn looks confused.

"Well, I sort of took a bus and then I was in the neighborhood. Um, by the way…" I gesture toward the side of her head.

"Oh, shit!" Autumn jams her hand into her bag. She takes out a wool knit cap and tugs it on over her head. "I keep forgetting," she says. "No magic, no glamour. At first I wondered if my ears might just go back to normal. But, nope."

"Weird," I say.

"Thanks."

I can't help laughing. "I didn't mean it that way. You know I like elf ears."

Autumn tugs at the cap again, looking around. "Did anybody see?"

"Don't worry about it," I say. "It's not like there's a law against having pointy ears."

Autumn starts walking again, and I fall in beside her. "True," she says. "But I didn't have pointy ears before, so that might seem a little strange."

I shrug. "Whatever. They'll get over it."

"Easy for you to say. You still have a glamour."

Which reminds me why I came stalking in the first place. We come to an intersection and I grab hold of Autumn's sleeve. I pull her around the corner.

"What the hell are you doing?"

Right, a little explanation might be nice. I'm acting like I'm trying to mug her. "Just hang on," I say. "I've got something for you."

Autumn lets me keep tugging on her until we step into an alley behind a restaurant. It smells like a grease trap back there, but at least no one is around. I pull the stone from my pocket. "Here. Maybe this will do the trick. Or at least *a trick*. I'm not sure."

Autumn stares at the Faerie stone, which glows blue in the palm of my hand. "What the heck is that?"

"A talisman," I say.

"Well, yeah, I can see that. Where did it come from?"

Does Autumn sound pissed? I could swear she sounds a little pissed. "I made it," I say. "Go on, give it a whirl."

Autumn shakes her head. "No."

"What do you mean, no? It took me like four hours to make this thing. At least give it a try. Maybe you can use it to cast a glamour."

Autumn sighs, but doesn't take the stone. "Look, that's really nice of you, but it's not worth the risk."

"What risk?"

"Of having you wind up in the same boat as me," Autumn says. "You don't get it, do you? What do you think will happen if they find out you shared your magic with me?"

She doesn't have to explain who she means by "they." Sarah Wellingsford and her masked henchmen, of course. "Screw them. What are they going to do about it?"

Autumn looks at me like I'm an idiot. "Um, I don't know. Maybe bind your powers and try to have you killed? All they need is an excuse."

"How do you know?"

Autumn sighs again. "Technically, I don't, but trust your gut. What do you think?"

I do as I've been told and arrive at the answer quickly. She's right. Sarah Wellingsford and her crowd would love nothing more than to take me out of the picture too. The only reason it hasn't happened already is because I was at that coven meeting. I just happen to have an alibi, when they probably counted on the opposite.

"I'm willing to take the risk," I say.

Autumn shakes her head. "Well, I'm not. I just couldn't live with it. Besides, right now you need your magic, and by that I mean all of it."

Knowing Autumn, I'm sure she means I need my magic to look after myself. At the same time, she just hammered another point home. If something happens to me, then how am I going to save her? Not to mention Bethany and the others. In other words, if I compromise my magic, or if Wellingsford takes me out of the picture, we're all screwed. No pressure or anything.

Still, I try one more time. "Are you sure?"

Autumn nods. "I'm sure."

I put the stone back into my pocket. "Then you should tell Ian. The two of you should just take off together. I'll find you guys after I clean up this mess."

Autumn doesn't even pretend to consider. "Not gonna happen. I'm not dragging him into this either. When it's over, I'll tell him. Okay?"

When it's over. By which she really means, *If I'm still around.* I fight back against tears yet again. This just isn't the time, and Autumn just doesn't need it. If she can handle this so calmly, then I can too.

I hesitate and then say, "Fair enough. You know he's going to be pissed, right?"

Autumn shrugs. "He's used to me. How'd it go with the vampire?"

"Nora?"

It's a stupid response. Who else could she mean?

Autumn raises an eyebrow. "That's her name?"

"Right, Nora."

Autumn thinks about that for a moment. "Huh. I always expect them to have names like Jessica and Victoria. You know, sort of gothic and creepy. Although, I guess that doesn't really make sense. Anyone can be turned into a vampire, I suppose."

Which I take to mean that soon there might be a vampire named Autumn.

To take her mind off of it, I say, "She seems nice."

Autumn's expression shifts to one of shock. "She's *nice?*"

"Well, she's a vampire, but she didn't try to kill me or anything."

I go on to tell Autumn about Nora, as well as a little about her history. I tell her about the other vampires I met, and what we've learned about Mason. For now, I leave out the dangers we encountered, promising myself that I really will tell her later. I know I told her I'd be transparent, but she just doesn't need the stress. I finish by saying that we plan to keep looking tonight.

Autumn glances at something behind me, then shifts her eyes back to mine. "Are you meeting her at that factory again?"

I hesitate, but then just go with the truth. After all, Autumn once took home a wounded werewolf. "She's at my place," I say.

Autumn's brow furrows with confusion. "Hang on. There's a vampire sleeping in your apartment?"

I shrug. "She promised not to feed on anyone. I think she'll keep her word." I glance at the darkening sky and add, "Besides, she's probably not up yet."

"Where did you put her?"

"In my closet," I say.

Autumn's expression shifts to one of amusement, and I get the feeling she's trying not to say something.

"What?" I say.

"So, you're saying you forced a gay vampire back into the closet."

We look at each other for a moment as I raise my eyebrows. Autumn stares at me with a smile tugging at her lips, and I have to laugh.

"Funny," I say.

Autumn shrugs. "I just couldn't resist." Then she glances behind me again, as if something keeps distracting her.

I turn around and see it too. Well, not it, him. He looks to be in his late forties or early fifties. He's a big man, mostly bald, wearing baggy gray trousers, a stained white t-shirt and an even more stained apron. He holds a spatula in one hand and a cigarette in the other. Apparently, the ghost cook just stepped out for a smoke break.

"Do you see him?" Autumn says.

I nod. "Plain as day."

Then I realize something. Even with her magic bound, Autumn still sees him. I have to wonder if maybe that part of a veil witch's magic can't be removed. Strangely, it's like the ghost only sees Autumn. I'm right next to her, but he stares at her with sad, tired eyes.

"Who are you?" he says.

"I'm Autumn."

He steps closer, his gaze remaining fixed on her. "I thought I was alone. I'm always alone back here."

"Not tonight." Autumn gestures toward the restaurant door. "I guess you must work there."

The cook nods, dragging deeply on his smoke. "It feels like this shift will never end. They just keep putting in more orders. Every time I catch up, it starts again. I swear, sometimes it feels like I'm going to have a heart attack."

As soon as he says it, I know, as I'm sure Autumn does too. The cook did have a heart attack. Long ago, right where we're standing.

Autumn speaks softly, her tone gentle. "I can make the shift end. Would you like that?"

The cook heaves out a weary sigh. "I'd really like to leave now," he says. "I just want to go home."

Autumn holds out her hand, just barely turning my way. "I'll give it right back," she whispers.

I know what she means, of course. I take the stone from my pocket and slip it into her waiting hand.

CHAPTER 12

Personally, I never wake up hungry, but apparently Nora does, so it's not long before we're once again hoofing through the city. Our destination isn't quite clear to me, but at least we're miles from the Cauldron. It's dicey enough keeping our presence masked from our neighbors. We definitely don't need adding a vampire to the mix.

"Are we almost there?" I say, trying not to sound winded.

"Getting there," Nora says. She turns to me and adds, "We've only been walking for an hour."

The implication being what? I'm lazy? Well, excuse me for having living legs. I ignore the comment and keep walking.

First on our agenda is Nora's breakfast. She just thinks better if she's not hungry, she says. Which, I suppose, is fair enough. I also learn that she rotates the places she goes to feed. Whether there's any particular pattern, she doesn't say, although I suppose that kind of thing would be good to know when hunting vampires.

I feel bad as soon as I think it, and then I try telling myself I shouldn't feel that way. After all, removing supernatural threats is my primary purpose. Should a cat feel bad about killing mice? No, right? They're supposed to kill mice. And sometimes it might even be a kindness releasing someone from their vampiric state. Many see it as a curse, a life spent living in the shadows, an existence driven by a constant thirst for blood. I wonder if I should ask Phoenix to pull off some necromancy and make contact with one of the vampires I killed. Just to check in, I guess. *Hey, dead vampire, any hard feelings?* Never mind. Probably not the best idea.

Still, it only takes that much to make me start thinking of Phoenix again. I picture that night last week at Isabel's house, and how natural it felt to be with him. I think of that moment when I reached for his hand, only to pull back again. In a sense, isn't that how I handled our relationship? I reached out to him, then gave myself to him, only to say I needed time alone. In other words, I freaked out at getting too close.

Wasn't it the same with Esras? Sure, I was all in for the sex, but then ran for the hills when he suggested commitment. Some of those concerns were legitimate, but the result was the same. As soon as I felt myself getting close, I bailed. Like really bailed, even telling myself I wouldn't go back to Faerie again. Now I know that was a lie, but why did I run to begin with?

Once again, I suspect my behavior is rooted in the trauma I suffered as a child. You can't exactly have your body snatched and not come away with trust issues. Still, talk about behavior patterns. It seems like I definitely have one myself. If a vampire ever wants to hunt this veil witch, all she has to do is head in the opposite direction of the guy who loves me.

Therapy, girl. Therapy.

Yes, I hear you, inner voice. How about this? Point out the therapist I can share my past with and I'll make that appointment.

Just more excuses, inner voice says. She always gets the last word.

"God, you're quiet tonight."

I actually jump at hearing Nora. For a moment, I forgot she was there. "Sorry," I say. "I kind of checked out there for a minute."

I look around to see that we just entered one of those Richmond neighborhoods comprised of small houses, rather than townhomes and apartment buildings. Sort of like a miniaturized suburb, the houses all one-story with their own little yards and garages. Although, our surroundings look a little run down, the houses worn and most of the cars and trucks old.

"Is this one of your spots?" I say.

Nora hesitates, and then says, "Yeah, one of them."

I suspect her hesitation resulted from the same thoughts that crossed my mind before. She's probably not sure how much to share with me. At some point our partnership will end. Then what?

Still, being naturally nosy, I say, "Why here?"

"Reasons," Nora says.

Is it me, or is she being snippy tonight? Do vampires get *hangry*?

Nora slows her pace, and then puts her arm out to stop me. Then I hear it too, a couple fighting inside a house across the street. They're not exactly being discreet.

A woman's voice cuts through the night, one with a Latino accent. "Why don't you try it, asshole? I'd like to see how you'd make out stuck here all day with three kids!"

"That's all you *gotta do!*" the guy hollers back. "Take care of the kids and keep the place clean!"

The woman's voice rises higher. "You think that's easy?"

The guy ups the stress level even more. "Try actually *working* sometime You just sit around and keep getting fatter!"

"Ouch," I say. "What an asshole."

"Shh."

Yes, the vampire shushes me, but it's like she knows what's about to happen. Soon the woman starts to cry. Which, of course, makes the man flee.

"Forget this!" he says. "I'm going out. This place better be cleaned up by the time I get back."

A moment later, a door slams as the guy comes out of the house. Beside me, Nora speaks softly. "Don't worry," she says. "I'll make sure he doesn't enjoy it."

Then she's gone, a shadow streaking through the night. The guy is almost to his car when she's upon him. Somehow, Nora keeps him from making a sound. From where I stand, I see just two silhouettes locked in an embrace. A moment later, those figures disappear as Nora takes her victim down to the ground.

~~~

Like last night, we decide to check out a few clubs, this time going inside to check out the scene. It's just the two of us, so there's no concern of anyone needing to feed. Each club is more or less the same, with music pounding and lights flashing as people dance, talk and stare at screens. I've never been a club-goer. In fact, I haven't been in one since that night when I first got back my powers and went on a supernatural rampage. It's probably for the best, I soon realize, since Nora's instincts prove right. In each club, I feel the kind of agitation telling me that vampires are present. The problem being that none of them are Mason.

As we leave the fourth club, I have to ask. "Is this what you do too?"

I keep the rest of the thought to myself, but what I'm thinking is how old it must get. It's one thing when you're young, killing time in places like that. Eventually, you get over it and move on. I can't imagine doing it for decades as you pretend to be what you once were.

"It seems kind of pathetic," Nora says. "Is that what you're thinking?"

"Yeah, sorry," I admit. "Maybe there's some part I don't understand."

She shakes her head. "No, you're pretty much seeing it for what it is. To answer your question, it really hasn't been this way for me. At least not much. Remember what I said about some vampires having the advantage of a group? Part of that is about protection, but not all of it. There's also the social aspect. At least for some groups. They become like family. After that, some of us don't feel so restless anymore."

I speak softly, feeling the sadness coming off of her. "So that's what it was like for you?"

Nora sighs. "Yes, it was."

I'm not sure if I should ask, but I've been curious. "Who were they?"

"There were five of us," Nora says. "Thomas, Joel, William, Emily and me. By the way, Emily and I were just friends. Just so you know."

There's just a slight edge to her voice, making me wonder if I pushed too far. Or maybe it's just too painful right now.

I don't know what to say, other than, "I'm sorry."

Nora looks over at me, her eyes flat and distant. "Thanks. Me too."

I understand the resentment in her gaze. How much can my sympathy mean to her? But the strangest thing is that her anger still hurts a little. Once again, guilt flares inside me.

As if knowing what I'm thinking about, Nora says. "Let's just keep looking. We need to get this done."

She's right. That's why we're here in the first place. What we are to each other after this isn't important. And it's quite possible, at some point in the future, we might just try to kill each other. That's just how the deal works.

~~~

The hour keeps growing later, the search getting us nowhere, while something keeps nagging at me. It's that thing I've been trying to ignore, and don't want to face again. Even thinking about it makes my heart beat faster. Still, it keeps bugging me. We need to know what drew those werewolves to Byrd Park.

For that reason, we're soon riding a bus across town, although Nora remains understandably reluctant.

"Seriously, are you *trying* to get us killed?"

It's the first time I've seen her look nervous. I understand. Vampires have almost no defense against werewolves.

"The full moon was last night," I say, trying to reassure her.

Nora points to the bus window, where a big round moon rides high in the sky. "Last night was the waxing full moon. That's the full moon right there. Also, werewolf magic isn't pinned to one night. It's just strongest on the full moon. Do you even know anything?"

Damn. She's right again, the brat. I keep proving myself to be a supernatural idiot. Did I actually save the Faerie realm a month ago? Maybe I just dreamt all that.

Still, I stick to my guns. "Okay, well, let me ask you this. Do werewolves usually prowl Byrd Park at night?"

Nora rolls her eyes. "Obviously not, or I wouldn't go there."

"Well, that's exactly what I'm getting at. Something had to cause that anomaly."

Nora thinks for a moment. "Maybe they were just chasing a deer or something."

I decide to let her believe that if it makes her feel better. "There you go. Then they shouldn't be there tonight."

Nora heaves out an epic sigh. "Fine. You better not get me killed."

I can't help but wonder if, to those around us, we might seem like sisters. In this case, me the older of the two. Weird. Although, I can easily imagine Autumn's eyes lighting up with amusement.

I look over at Nora, who's turned to the window as she stares up at the moon. "I won't get you killed."

"You better not," Nora says.

This time, I imagine Autumn laughing.

~~~

It's past two by the time we enter the park, that full moon still shining brightly above. Yes, it's beautiful, but it's also a big fat reminder that this is a night prime for werewolf magic.

Not surprisingly, Nora is on edge too as we keep venturing further. She walks without making a sound, her head swiveling as she continues to scan. As she looks away from me, I resist the urge to tap her shoulder and say, "Boo!" It's ridiculous, for one thing, but she's also fast as shit. Those fangs of hers might hit my neck before I finish laughing.

"See anything?" I say.

Nora points and says, "Just a homeless guy over there. Too bad I'm not hungry."

"I probably freaked the furry bastards out last night. Maybe they're scared to come back."

Nora keeps looking around. "Yeah, let's hope."

Byrd Park is a large public space, over two hundred acres across. It has three lakes, hiking paths, running trails and sports fields. There's also an amphitheater and a number of monuments. The crown jewel is the Carillon bell tower, which rises hundreds of feet into the sky. It's toward that tower that we now walk, drawn partly by its size I suppose. Still, there's no denying the agitation I feel as we get closer. It starts as a mild tingling at the back of my neck, soon intensifying to travel down through my arms toward my hands. My body's way of telling me I'll soon need magic.

A quick check shows that nothing has changed for Nora. If anything, she seems more at ease now that we haven't seen any werewolves. I'm pretty sure she's right too. I'm not sensing werewolves, but I'm definitely sensing vampires. And, if I'm not wrong, I'm sensing a lot of them.

CHAPTER 13

Instinctively, I reach out and grab hold of Nora's arm. It's a strange moment in several ways. First of all, I've never touched a vampire. Magic flares inside me, my solar plexus lighting up with heat. In contrast, no heat comes off her at all. Even through the sleeve of her jacket, I can tell she holds no warmth. I might as well have touched a statue. On top of that, I take her completely by surprise. Much like I'd imagined before, she rears back to expose fangs that have instantly descended.

"Sorry," I whisper. "I didn't mean to scare you."

"Damnit!" Nora says. "You scared the crap out of me. What's going on?"

I point toward the tower, which looms close now. But that's all I see, just the tower and the shadowy trees surrounding it.

"You don't see anything?" I say.

Nora shifts her gaze in that direction, frowning as she stares into the night. She shakes her head. "What should I see?"

There was no reason to think she should—after all, I don't sense other witches—but clearly she doesn't feel what I feel. Obviously, she doesn't see anything either.

"Vampires," I say. "I can feel them. They're somewhere nearby."

I guess just to be sure, Nora scans all around us. Once more, she shakes her head. "I don't see anyone. Are you sure?"

"Definitely."

It makes no sense, what I'm experiencing. How can I feel vampires this strongly—every fiber of my being telling me they're nearby—when there's no sign of them? If I was alone, I might convince myself that it was just about lacking night vision. That's not the problem, obviously. Nora stands right next to me, and I know she wouldn't lie.

Suddenly, I realize what's going on. As Julia pointed out, my senses keep getting stronger. They extend farther than they used to. Even, quite possibly, past this very realm.

I turn to Nora again. "You said before that vampires can go to the Inversion. Are you sure about that?"

She doesn't hesitate. "Absolutely."

"You said there are portals, right? Doorways you guys can use to get there?"

"That's what I've been told," Nora says, "I have no idea where they are."

She looks around again, her nervousness starting to grow. Clearly, she doesn't like where this is going. Her instincts are sound. I don't like where it's going either. More importantly, I *really* don't like where I think we're both going.

"Come on!" I start toward the tower, striding fast, soon close to running. It's definitely the first time Nora has had to catch up with me.

"Talk to me, Cassie. What are you thinking?"

Yeah, she must be scared. That's the first time she's used my name. I pick up my pace even more.

"I'm thinking we're near one of those portals. We need to find it."

Nora abruptly stops, this time latching onto me. I wheel about as I get thrown off balance, my arm socket objecting to the tug. She may be small, but she's vampire-strong. If she'd wanted to, she could have torn my arm off.

"Are you freaking crazy?" she says.

I shrug. "Kind of. Sometimes. Can I have my arm back?"

Nora reluctantly lets go, her eyes glowing in the darkness.

I step back. "You said you wanted to avenge your friends. Did you change your mind?"

She shakes her head.

"Good," I say. "Because I'd like to keep my sister alive. So let's find the freaking portal, open it and find out what the hell is going on."

I don't wait for her to agree. I turn and start walking again, not looking back until we reach the Carillon. My core thrums with an energy lighting up every nerve ending. Then another sensation is added to the mix, as my skin starts to crawl. I've never felt this sensation before, not exactly. But I suspect it's what I'd feel if I came upon a combined group of demons and vampires. Only, I'm not yet seeing what I'm feeling. I take one last moment to consider what Nora said before. Maybe I am crazy. I'd have to be to do what I'm about to attempt.

I take a deep breath and extend my supernatural feelers. It takes a few moments, and even then I don't see it. Instead, it's what I hear that shows me the way forward. I once told Grayson that I could hear wards, and he was hesitant to believe me. All the same, it's true, at least sometimes. This is one of those times, as a low humming starts to rise inside my ears. It sounds like it's coming from the earth. I tune in more and then feel it too, my body vibrating at its core.

I turn to Nora and whisper, "It's in back, behind the tower."

She nods, her eyes frightened. I start walking and she follows.

Behind the tower, I perceive only darkness, and for a moment I think it might be the angle of the moon. Instinctively, I know it's more than that. We're not facing shadows, or a place merely beyond the reach of moonlight. Unlike the shimmering portal to Faerie, we face a gap like an inky void. As the thrumming keeps traveling up through the ground, I make the connection. I think of that night when I was in the Inversion, and how I flew through the sky. At one point, I saw massive structures of stone, and I realized they'd always been there, remaining cloaked by some ancient magic.

Trusting the ancient magic within myself—that of my veil witch bloodline—I command my vision to shift. Only then do I see the dimmest of outlines, the black on black seam of a door. Now that I've found it, that seam shifts from black to gray, allowing through the faintest of light. Then gray shifts to purple, then starts to glow red. Still, that doorway won't open.

In a moment of certainty, I also know why.

I turn to Nora and say, "It has to be you."

Her eyes meet mine, and I see that she both knows and she's terrified. I want to tell her to think of her lost friends. Thomas and Joel. William and Emily. I want to remind her of how much she lost. Instead, I don't speak and I wait.

Finally, Nora nods. I was right, in that this is ancient magic. But it's one that yields only to vampires. She walks forth and raises her hand. From the top down, a hole in the world melts open, emitting a fiery glow. We hesitate one last time, and then we step through.

CHAPTER 14

The scene shifts around us, the bell tower and park vanishing as the light shifts to hues of orange and red. We stand before the steps of a massive structure that looks like an ancient temple, with walls and columns of stone. Two giant doors stand open, casting a fiery glow from within.

I look around just long enough to detect that, if we're in the same geographical space, you'd never know it. Gone is the distant city skyline, along with the sound of human life. Awash in red-tinted moonlight, the land stretches as far as the eye can see, a rolling expanse of hills. It's like we've stepped back in time—maybe five hundred years, or even a thousand—into what this place might have once been.

"We should go," Nora says. "Come back when we have a plan. I have a bad feeling about this."

There's no doubt that I'm nervous too. I break out in a sweat as I think of the high demon I faced before. I picture her rising into the sky, electricity sizzling around her as she cradles fire in her hand.

I force the image from my mind and start climbing the steps. "I'll just take a quick look."

Nora's breathless voice comes from behind me. "Hang on, I'm coming with you."

I figured she probably would. Nora hasn't backed off yet. Even when we faced that bull demon last night, she stood beside me.

If I was agitated before, I'm all but on fire by the time we climb the steps to enter a massive antechamber, with walls arching to meet a ceiling far above our heads. To our right there's an alcove, within it a staircase descending into darkness. We step forward, remaining in the shadows as we approach another set of doors.

For a moment, I stand stunned and motionless, too shocked to process what I see. Not because it can't be real, but because I'd hoped it couldn't be. It's as if I've walked into my nightmare. At least fifty vampires stand before an altar. I see demons too, those same elongated creatures that the high demon called drudes. I also see humans bound to the wall.

As in my dream, they're not held by chains. Red tendrils of magic are roped around their arms, legs and torsos. There are at least a dozen of them, both men and women, each dressed in a sheer white robe. The only thing different from my dream is that they don't stare out with terrified eyes. Instead, they gaze vacantly, as if unaware of their surroundings.

Beside me, Nora whispers, "It's the Shared Feast."

I knew, of course. All the same, nothing could have prepared me.

The vampires line up and start walking forward. One at a time, they step up onto the altar, each taking a turn with one of the victims. My eyes widen in horror at the sight of bloody mouths and white gowns starting to streak with scarlet. The demons open their own gaping mouths, their grotesque bodies shuddering with pleasure as they feed upon the energy.

Then I just can't take any more. The magic I've been holding at bay floods through me, a burning heat surging toward my hands. Even the athame strapped to my calf hums against my skin, as magic pours into its blade.

I start to step forward but Nora's iron grip latches onto my arm. She yanks me back, her urgent gaze locking onto mine. She's right. I need to calm down, and this isn't the moment to strike.

Suddenly, a man starts to speak where the vampires congregate, his voice resonating throughout the stone chamber. "These willing supplicants won't remember what takes place here tonight. For now, it serves our purposes that they forget having been here."

I realize that only my initial shock at the scene could have kept me from seeing him before. He's taller than most of the others, thin and broad-shouldered in a long black coat. He has long dark hair and keen brown eyes that survey those around him. He spreads his arms and grins, his fangs having descended for the feeding.

"Let the humans think they've chased us into the shadows. Let them believe we no longer exist. Either is fine." His grin broadens as he gestures to those held bound, their blood being drained. "Let a few fools believe that they can make deals with our demon friends. Let them continue to believe they're in control. Let them think that, only when doing their bidding, can the demons step forward into their realm." His voice rises in both intensity and volume. "Let them believe all of this to be true. Because we know differently. The time is at hand when we won't fear them or the sun under which they walk. We will open the gates and blot that sun out. We will take back what's meant to be ours, and be revered like gods. Feared! Immortal! Unstoppable!"

Holy shit. This guy's nuts.

Apparently, my sentiment isn't shared by the vampires, whose approving voices rise in unison. Cheers echo off the walls. One of the feeding vampires even drags his fangs out of his victim to cry out in agreement. Blood drains from his mouth as he pumps his fist in the air. It's not just my nightmare; it's my nightmare on steroids. But, still, it's just crazy. Do they seriously think that by aligning themselves with the demons they can take down our realm?

Then an icy chill overcomes me, because they may not be wrong. They haven't just aligned themselves with the demons. They also have a veil witch on their side, one who is gaining strength by the day. I strongly suspect there's a deeper reason why that strength keeps growing. A reason I've been told isn't possible, but I still can't ignore what I feel. Especially because if I'm right, then it's not just one realm trying to break through to ours; it's possibly two.

Another tug on my arm snaps me out of it. Nora is more gentle this time, but not by much. The pain of her grip shoots through me as I spin to face her.

"We need to go," she whispers.

I shake my head, stubborn as always. I need to remain here and figure out what to do.

Nora's eyes flare wide. She whispers louder, more insistently. *"We need to go!"*

It's only when she gestures behind us, to the doorway leading outside, that I understand her sudden panic. It's dark beyond those doors when it shouldn't be. We're in the Inversion, which means the sky should glow orange. A shadow has descended and I'm pretty sure I know who's out there. Ice cold fear ripples through me as I recall feeling hunted and helpless, the high demon swooping in upon me from the sky.

I grab hold of Nora and point her toward the stairwell. I hiss out the word, "Run!"

Then we run toward the stairs, looking for a place to hide. It may be our only hope, if we have any at all.

CHAPTER 15

We plunge into darkness, having no idea what waits below. The staircase curves along the stone wall, with no railing to keep me from falling. If I do, who knows how far I might drop. Then Nora steps in beside me to take the outside. Is she doing it to protect me because she can see? There's no time to ask as we keep running, my heart pounding and my breath coming in ragged gasps. Nora makes no sound at all.

Finally, my feet strike level stone, the impact traveling painfully up my shins. I lurch forward, starting to stumble when Nora grabs hold of me once more. I still can't see a thing, my eyes unable to adjust. That doesn't keep me from feeling a force closing in from all sides.

"What do you see?" I whisper.

A moment passes and then Nora says, "Not much."

Oh, shit. Even she can't see down here?

But then she whispers, "Shadows. At least I think they're shadows."

"How many? How big are they?"

"Too many to count. Huge. I think. There's nothing *but* shadows." She sounds panicked, close to losing control.

Then those shadows wrap themselves around me. Snakelike tendrils grab hold of my arms and legs while others coil around my waist. Smaller tendrils slither into my ears, nose and mouth. I shudder and struggle as, at the back of my mind, I hear the word "shades." Whether that's some ancient witch instinct speaking, I just don't know, but I've heard of shades before. Strangely, I thought they were from Faerie. Apparently not, since clearly they're demons. That's as far as I get before the darkness wraps around my brain.

Terror rises inside me as images of everything that's ever frightened me start flashing through my mind, as the demon magic taps into my fears. It finds Opal, that monster who stole my body. It finds the demons, evil spirits and vampires I've faced. Then there's Vintain's bone-white face leering close to mine. I soon learn that the darkness doesn't have to make do with what's actually happened, as it burrows deeper and deeper. I struggle but can't move, like a poisoned fly caught in a web. I thrash and shake my head, trying to fight, but it still finds what it's looking for. Images of Autumn flash before me. She's helpless and stripped of magic, vampires about to close in around her. I hear her flesh ripping and her bones breaking. Her screams rise in agony as they tear her apart.

From the recesses of my brain, I hear Beatrice's words. *The more we suffer, the stronger they grow.*

Still, I remain overwhelmed and powerless, even the sound of my own screams not breaking the spell. Then, from what feels like a million miles away, another sound manages to cut through. I hear Nora cry out in desperate terror. She may be a vampire now, but her pleas are those of a young woman.

"Stop, you're killing her!" she wails. "I'm begging you. *Please!*"

I can't be sure what she's experiencing, but I can pretty well guess. It's her pain which galvanizes my resolve, making me remember what I am and why I came here. Before I succumb once more, I summon my magic, pulling up all that I have. The tendrils release me as the fire lights up in my core. I stumble back, freed and gasping for air. Before the shades can encroach again, I light up an energy whip and lash out. The shades withdraw more, twisting like smoke, pulling back to remain out of reach.

Beside me, Nora kneels on the floor, her back convulsing and her hands pressed to the stone. I strike out at the demons surrounding her, making them too pull away. But within this massive chamber, they have plenty of room. Time seems no issue for them either, as they wait for me to tire and weaken.

I barely dare look at Nora as I keep lashing out. "Talk to me. Are you okay?"

She groans, and from the corner of my eye I see her rise to her feet. A few moments pass before she yells, "I don't think it's working!"

"I know!" Still, I keep spinning and striking, my efforts all but futile. How long can I keep this up? Not long enough, obviously. Even if I kept on for a year, the shades would still be there. Unlike me, they're not physical creatures. They're comprised solely of malevolent energy.

"Cassie, look out!"

I pivot just in time to hit a shade that was sneaking in from behind. It dissolves and swirls back once more. I might as well be battling mist.

Suddenly, Nora cries out in anguish as she's again overtaken. I scream out, "Get away from her!" I snap the whip over and over as the same thought keeps repeating. *I need more magic. I need more magic.*

I grit my teeth and slash the whip in one great final arc to buy myself some time. *Come on, come on, come on!* What the hell can I do? I think of the Faerie ley line, but it's a desperate thought. I'm not in her realm and I can't expect her to help me. But thinking of her makes me connect with something else I'd forgotten—the Faerie stone still in the pocket of my jeans.

I wrap my hand around the stone, commanding it to give me all the power stored within it. A sudden surge of magic flows through me, forcing me to clench my eyes shut as my back involuntarily arches. This time when Nora cries out, I know it's because of me.

My eyes pop open to a room so brilliantly bright that it's difficult to withstand. Each of my hands blazes with crackling energy, two times at least what I used against the werewolves. Damn, nice boost.

"Stop! *Please stop!*"

I have no choice but to ignore Nora's cries as I search our surroundings. I see the chamber now, vast and high. Its walls seem alive as the shades cling to it, slithering over each other as they try to escape. I have four walls to choose from, so I choose the one with the stairs that carried us down here. That has to be an outside wall.

My eyes turn to slits as I stare at the wriggling forms. I call out, "*You want out of here, you fuckers! Well, here you go!*" I thrust out both hands, light surging from me as the wall explodes outward. Flaming boulders shoot through the air as a cloud of dust blooms and then billows.

Nora remains huddled on the ground, but I drag her to her feet and then guide her as we run across the chamber. We clear the now gaping wall, stumbling as we make our way outside.

"Open your eyes," I say. "We're safe!"

No sooner do I say it when something blocks out the light of the moon. Another shadow descends, this one taking on the form of a woman.

CHAPTER 16

She's just as I remember from my nightmares. Stunningly beautiful, tall and graceful with high cheekbones and full lips. Like last time, she wears a sheer dress accentuating her form. Her amber eyes glow and her ruby hair seems woven from this realm's vermilion moonlight. She strides toward me, barely glancing at Nora.

Her lips curl up at their corners in an amused smile. "So, we meet again. Didn't I warn you that I'd know if you came here?"

I heave out a breath, tired from the last fight. Does this shit never stop? "Yeah, you told me. I came anyway. Do you have a name, or what?"

She tilts her head thoughtfully. "Did you think I'd be afraid to tell you? That perhaps knowing would give you power over me?"

I shrug. "Honestly, that never occurred to me. Is that even a thing?"

"Only in storybooks," she says, her eyes growing even more amused.

"Yeah, well, I thought witches only existed in storybooks too." I shrug again. "But look at me now."

To my surprise, she laughs, the sound somehow both warm and frightening. "Yes, look at you now. Ever curious. Always pushing the boundaries."

I stick to my guns. It's just been bugging me. "So, the name," I say. "I just like to know who I'm talking to."

"As you wish," she says. "My name is Nepheras."

I shake my head. "Seriously? That sounds like a nasal spray. Are you effective against ragweed?"

Sure, I'm pushing it, but it's not like we're striking up a friendship. It's only a matter of moments before we try to kill each other.

Once again, she surprises me, this time with a casual shrug. "To your ears, my name might sound strange. For the record, *Cassie* isn't exactly music to mine."

She puts just the right emphasis on my name to make it sound like part of a toilet bowl. Damn, this chick's good.

"How do you feel about Cassandra?"

She shakes her head. "Even worse."

Yeah, same here, so I really can't argue. I gesture to the temple behind us. "I might have damaged your house. Not to mention your living wallpaper."

Nepheras seems entirely unbothered. "Shades have a way of recovering quickly. You'd be amazed at their resilience."

As we trade barbs, it's like Nora isn't even here. Apparently, Nepheras isn't worried about her. Either way, I don't dare tear my eyes away from Nepheras as she starts closing the distance between us. Her pace is relaxed, her expression calm and knowing.

Like last time, ozone builds in the air, the pressure rising. Nepheras's hair floats upward to fan out around her face. Her eyes shift from amber to fiery golden. Her smile is replaced by a grin displaying two rows of pointed teeth. If the effect is meant to frighten me, it definitely works. She just went from beautiful to terrifying in three seconds flat.

Thankfully, I've seen more than my share of frightening things. I've gone up against vampires, body-snatchers and powerful dark witches. I've defeated evil fae queens and mages. What's another demon, right?

That's what I tell myself, struggling to stay calm as Nepheras spreads her hands to the air. The ozone pressure builds even more. I feel my own hair lifting, as static crackles around me. Wait, can she actually—?

I dodge as a lightning bolt strikes down to explode in a white-hot flash, the spot where I just stood reduced to a smoldering hole. My mind reels as I recall the word that came to me last time. *Goddess.*

No way. She can't possibly be a—

I dart away just in time to avoid another lightning strike, the ground exploding as dirt and rock spray. Come on. Seriously? I'd almost managed to convince myself that the first strike had been a coincidence. But, whatever, she just missed twice.

Nepheras shrugs, as if hearing my thoughts. "Just warming up," she says.

Another lightning bolt strikes down, followed by another in a quick succession of blinding flashes. Nepheras laughs as I dodge and scurry. She keeps laughing as more bolts follow, each one getting closer. I hate to be selfish, but if she'd just spend a little time on Nora, then maybe I could muster up some magic to strike back. As it is, I can barely manage to keep from getting fried as I circle what amounts to an electrified cage. No wonder Nepheras keeps laughing. I must look ridiculous. I also get the feeling she's almost done toying with me.

Another lightning bolt strikes down, and this time I drop, flip and roll, hoping to break the pattern. I spring to my feet where Nepheras doesn't anticipate and the next bolt wildly misses. It takes her only a moment to recalibrate, but at least it gives me time to invoke a shielding spell.

That's as far as I get before the strikes resume. One would have baked me for sure, but instead it explodes in a shower of sparks against my shield.

"Well, look at that!" Nepheras says. "See, you're getting better!"

Seriously, the bitch is mocking me now?

"You haven't seen anything yet," I say, spitting out the words through gritted teeth.

"Definitely true," Nepheras says.

I freaking hate this demon. If she's a god, no wonder the human race ran them out of town. The annoyance factor alone would inspire millions to sacrifice themselves in battle.

I try to call up more magic as Nepheras lights up the sky once more. Her strikes start up again, jagged arcs of fire streaking down to pound against my shield. There's no way I'm going to last much longer.

The barrage suddenly stops as Nepheras lets out a scream of pain, her face contorting into a shocked mask of rage. She staggers and spins in the moonlight, clutching at the knife in her back. Then a shadow streaks out from behind her, moving toward me like a bat out of hell.

"Get us out of here, veil witch!"

I'm already on it, the shield gone and a bluish-white orb expanding in my hand. I open the veil and Nora darts through the gap with me right behind her. The two of us stumble out into Byrd Park, where I trip and fall to the ground. Then I jump up again, spin around and make damned sure to close the veil behind us.

CHAPTER 17

The next afternoon I'm still groggy as I trudge across the field getting ready for practice session part two. Once we're back in place, the four of us lined up like boot camp cadets, Regina hovers before us like a fat little bee. I really wish she didn't make it look so easy.

"For this afternoon's entertainment," she bellows, "you'll pair off against each other!"

She pauses just long enough for us to volley apprehensive glances back and forth.

Then she continues. "That way, you can really learn what your opponent is made of. You'll need to know, if you're going to have each other's backs in battle. And, as you've probably surmised, one is likely soon coming."

Regina's referring to the same incident that inspired today's grueling regimen. Evidently, during my visit to the Inversion last night, the veil was once again breached. This time, out by the airport. Why there, I have no idea, but social media soon lit up with reports of gremlins seen on the wings of a departing flight. Of course, those claims were dismissed, and the emergency landing blamed on an engine malfunction. Still, we know better.

And I care. I really do, but what a day for our first double-header. The four of us—well, five including Regina—already put in four hours before lunch. It rained this morning, so my boots are muddy and my clothes sticking to my skin. I'm also still beat from my death match with Nepheras. At least I didn't leave a vampire in my closet, so that part's good. After we made it out of the Inversion last night, Nora called Stephanie to see if she could stay there. Maybe she figured I was dangerously impulsive, or maybe she just didn't want to spend another night in my closet, not to mention a building full of witches. She didn't say.

Still, it was a long night, and it took everything I had to drag myself here this morning. Right now, all I want is a cup of mint tea and a nice hot bath.

I'm snapped out of that fantasy by Regina screaming in my face. "Am I boring you, Ms. Anderson?"

Yes, she loves to repeat my generic surname. It's her way of putting me in my place. With Autumn's powers on ice, we all know what the stakes are. At some point, it will come down to me. No pressure or anything.

"Sorry, just a little tired," I say. "Is this really necessary?"

Not surprisingly, Regina doesn't react well to my question. "Is this *necessary*? You're *tired*? Well, excuse me, Ms. Anderson, but some of us believe this is very necessary. As in, we need to protect the human race! Are you not on board?"

Oh, fucking hell. Will I ever learn to keep my mouth shut? Sadly, probably not. My face grows hot as I look around at the others. "Yes, I'm very much on board. Sorry."

"Good!" Spittle flies into my face as Regina hovers before me. "Can we get back to practice?"

"Yes, of course. I was just—"

"Harper, you work with Blair!" Regina bellows. "Alec! You pair off against this one!"

Great, that should really help the dynamic between us.

Regina buzzes over to where she left what looks like a lunch box sitting in the grass. I was kind of hoping she brought snacks, but once again she doesn't fail to disappoint. She flips open the case to reveal that it's lined with foam, from which protrude four glass tubes. She plucks those out and zooms back in our direction, passing one to each of us. The tubes contain a murky substance roughly the color of poop.

"Those are for you to drink," Regina informs us, apparently assuming there's no need for further explanation.

Huh?

"What is it?" Blair says.

Thank you, Blair.

"A potion," Regina says.

I feel like pointing out that we weren't drafted. Technically, we didn't even enlist. We could leave if we feel like it. I don't say this because I'm afraid to.

"What does it do?" Harper asks.

127

Thank you, Harper.

Regina glares at her. "Do I sense a trust issue?" However, before Harper can respond, Regina adds, "But fine. If you must know, these vials contain an inhibitor potion. For non-magical humans, the result would be displaying more inhibited behavior, the subject most typically questioning the effectiveness of their default settings. The jokester would be less sure about making a joke, the flirt less likely to bat her eyes, et cetera. The potion was developed to break habits and inspire new behaviors."

Regina stares at us as if we should be good to go.

"What about us?" I say, risking more scorn.

She sighs with impatience. "For witches, drinking this potion will keep you from reaching for your most handy trick, that thing you rely on as your default defense tactic. It's time to strengthen those secondary skills. Now drink!"

While I'm not excited about drinking Regina's potion, I guess it won't kill me. Then again, she handed each of us a specific vial. I mean, she wouldn't, right? I think about asking Alec to trade, but his vial is already empty. The same goes for Harper and Blair. Regina continues staring as she waits. *Yes, Regina, you do detect a trust issue.*

Screw it. I swallow the potion, which actually tastes like pomegranate and lime. Huh. How about that? I brace myself for whatever is supposed to happen, but it seems like nothing does. I have to wonder if it might be a magical dud.

Regina points down the field, to where two large circles are outlined with stones. They weren't there before, but that doesn't surprise me. I've gotten used to the practice field transforming at Regina's will. "Blair and Harper, take the circle on the left." She turns to us and says, "Alec and Anderson, you take the one on the right."

Love you too, Regina.

We do as we're told, crossing the field to take our places.

"Okay, have at it, Regina says.

Blair sighs, rolling smoky eyes ringed with black makeup. "What does that even mean?"

Regina lifts into the air. "It means magically subdue your opponent. Starting now!" She blows through a whistle that suddenly appears in her mouth, making sure to direct its shrill blast at my ear.

Then Alec and I stare at each other, having no idea what to do. I glance over to see Harper and Blair shifting listlessly too.

"Okay, how about a little incentive?" Regina calls out. "First one out of their circle gets to call it a day. The loser stays for three more hours."

Okay, bath, here I come....

Regina blows into her whistle again, making me wince. "By the way, you can't leave your circle while your opponent is still standing. And don't hold back. We have healers who can address most injuries."

Most? Comforting.

Still, it sounds easy enough. All I have to do is take Alec down and then skedaddle. As soon as I entertain that thought, the stones marking our boundary rise up into the air and start whizzing around the perimeter of the circle. Oh, come on! That's ridiculous. There's no way to get past that without having your head bashed in. Screw this.

Suddenly the stones freeze midair, hanging suspended for a few seconds before they start spinning again. Clever girl. Regina is making it tough, but not impossible. The right combat skill, combined with the right timing, and it's tea time for me.

I shift my attention back to Alec. He shrugs as if to say, *Sorry, but I have to kick your ass now.*

Obviously, this dude has no idea who I went up against last night.

We start circling each other, Alec going into his terramancy stance at the same time I go to light up an energy whip. I figure a few well-placed lashes will bring him to his knees. My guess is that he's planning to snare me with one of his vine traps. With me immobilized he'll be good to go. Neither happens.

For a moment, Alec and I both look at each other with bewildered expressions. Then I realize what's going on. Oh, right. Our default settings have been disabled. Time to use those secondary skills. I can tell Alec is thinking the same thing.

"What are you waiting for?"

Presumably, Regina is shouting at the two of us, but I don't dare take my eyes off of Alec. It's ridiculous, but we both start to circle each other again like a couple of sumo wrestlers. I'm not sure what he's up to, but I'm trying to think. Secondary skills, secondary skills…

Geez, Regina may have a point. Everything I do involves energy manipulation. Sure, it's powerful, but maybe it's time to think outside the box. Okay, I can also open the veil, but that must be rooted in the same magic. Besides, even my primary magic isn't always effective when facing an opponent. Last night, for example. I couldn't exactly bounce Nepheras out of the Inversion. Why would I want to? Just the opposite. She needs to either stay there or die. Preferably the latter. Either way, my other powers were essentially useless against her. Honestly, I have no idea what kind of power would match her own but—

Where the hell did Alec go? I only just realize he's gone when something shoves me from behind. I stumble forward, almost losing my balance, and then whirl around to see Alec grinning at me.

"Did you just shove me?"

He shrugs with a lopsided grin. "You know the rules."

Okay, fair enough. He can't leave while I remain on my feet. Regardless, who cares? How the hell did he just do that?

We resume circling as I try to think. What else do I have in my arsenal? Well, I can blind someone with intense light. But that's still energy magic. I'm kind of psychic sometimes, but that's useless right now.

Suddenly, Alec blips out of existence again. A split-second later I get shoved from the side, nearly going down this time. I stumble sideways thinking, *What the hell?* And, yes, Alec is grinning once more.

He starts circling again, so I do the same. Is he freaking enjoying this? I swear he's—

A quick flash, no Alec, then another shove, this time from the other side. Fucking bastard! Is he freaking teleporting? He is, isn't he?

"If you just drop, we can go home," Alec says. "Well, I can anyway."

We resume circling, this time my blood boiling. I stare daggers at the entitled, pedigreed, fancy-witch-school-trained little shit across from me. Speaking of daggers, what about my athame? Okay, I'm pissed off, but I'm not pissed off enough to stab him. Am I?

Alec blips out and I keep circling, waiting for him to reappear. Suddenly, two things occur to me. He's shoved me once from behind and once from each side. I bet anything he'll reappear to attack from behind. The other thing is that, while I'm light years behind Regina, I pulled off levitation the other day. Just briefly, but, hey.

With that in mind, I jump up and manage to stay floating as I spin around. Sure enough, Alec appears exactly where I thought he would. Only this time, I'm both facing him and hovering above the ground. I angle back, pull both knees to my stomach and plant a two-legged mule kick into Alec's chest. He lets out a painful groan as the wind rushes from his lungs. Then he stumbles back and falls on his ass. And it must be my lucky day, because the stones freeze mid-air in that same moment. I dash through just before they start spinning again.

Alec stares back at me, both stunned and angry. He croaks out, "What's your deal?"

He does have a point, in that I returned playful shoves with a full-on frontal assault. Hopefully, I didn't break any ribs.

Still, I just shrug. "You knew the rules."

There it is again, Alec bringing out the worst in me. I start walking toward the castle, looking over my shoulder to see Harper and Blair are still circling. Harper doesn't appear to be experiencing hallucinations, and Blair's not on fire, so I guess they're still digging around in their magical toolkits. As for Regina, she watches me with a curious expression. If I didn't know better, I might even think she's impressed.

Right now, I really don't care. I'm exhausted. And while part of me feels like I owe Alec an apology, I'm just not up for it now. All I want to do is go home. So, of course, a shadow falls over me. I look up to see Regina hovering overhead.

"Anderson, Beatrice said she wanted to speak to you before you left. I figured that would be hours from now."

Well, thank you very much, Regina.

"Meet her in the sitting room."

As if to remind me that I'm a toddler at levitation, she swings around in a graceful arc before shooting back toward the others. She does this while yawning and checking her phone. Show off.

~~~

Beatrice waits in the same sitting room where we first talked the other day. When I arrive, she waves me in and then gestures to a chair across from her. I take a seat as she floats a vial of blue liquid across the coffee table between us. It waits suspended in the air.

"To counter the inhibitor," Beatrice says. "If you prefer, you can just wait until it wears off. Probably a few hours, at best."

Yeah, not happening. Levitation will only get me out of so many squeezes. I reach for the vial, pull out the cork and suck back the contents. The potion tastes kind of like buttered toast with cinnamon. Not bad.

Watching me, Beatrice nods. "That's what I thought. Not having access to your primary magic can be an uncomfortable experience."

The vial starts wiggling in my hand, as if trying to escape.

Beatrice notices my confused expression. "You can let go."

I do and the vial floats up to puff out of existence in a cloud of blue vapor.

"Something we've been working on," Beatrice says, a pleased smile curving her lips. "Quantum glass. One step better than recycling."

Pretty nifty, I have to admit, but I'm distracted by a sudden shift from feeling exhausted to downright perky. I gesture to where the vial just vaporized. "Was there something else in there?"

"A little pick me up," Beatrice says. "Entirely organic, I assure you. You must be tired." Her eyes meet mine and she adds, "Ellis spoke to Nora this morning. He called her a little before sunrise."

Oh.

The thing is, I saw Beatrice earlier but didn't mention going to the Inversion. I wasn't sure how that would go over, considering I wasn't even close to having a plan at the time. I figure I can work my way around to it when the time feels right.

Then Beatrice continues. "Nora said the two of you got into a bit of a scrape."

So much for holding those cards close to my vest. I sigh and run my hand through my hair. "I have to admit it was touch and go there for a minute."

I stop short of saying Nora saved my life, but essentially she did. So, there's another one I never would have expected, that Nora carries a blade. Well, carried. The last time I saw her knife, it was sticking out of Nepheras's back. I didn't think vampires felt the need to carry weapons, but I guess being lightning fast and having fangs won't always do the trick.

I also realize that Nora didn't need me to leave the Inversion. She's a vampire, and apparently they're allowed to come and go. She knew where that portal was, so I guess she could have just run off and left me. She chose not to do that.

"Yes, she said it was close," Beatrice says, keeping me in her penetrating gaze. "I understand you encountered a high demon."

I shrug, mostly to keep myself from feeling freaked out at the memory. "Turns out I did."

"And?"

"You weren't wrong about them making a strong first impression." Well, technically second, but there's no point in going into that now. "So, what's the deal? Are they, like, gods or something?"

Beatrice tilts her head. "An interesting question. Do you believe in gods?"

I consider for a moment. "I always figured they were myth."

Beatrice raises an eyebrow. "And witches?"

Funny she should ask, because it parallels my thought from last night. "I didn't before, but I do now."

"Exactly," Beatrice says. "Of course you do, because you're one yourself. Before that, presumably, you also assumed witches to be myth. Now, you know witches can bend physics, literally command the natural elements around them."

"Not like her," I say.

Beatrice shrugs. "Don't underestimate yourself. You're still learning. But to answer your question, yes. High demons were once considered to be gods. This realm we live in has traded hands a few times, its history much different than that perceived by our non-magical counterparts. Not that their science is wrong with regard to the physical plane. However, we both know that's just the tip of the iceberg. All these dimensions wrapped around themselves can be quite the conundrum. Regardless, right now we need to focus on the realm we're trying to protect. Which brings us to the risk you took last night. Was it worth it?

The strange thing is, I don't hesitate. "Definitely. We know what's going on now."

Since the cat is out of the bag, I tell Beatrice about what happened last night, how we returned to Byrd Park because of the werewolves, about discovering the portal and entering the temple to witness the Shared Feast, as well as what we heard Mason say to those gathered there. Which brings me to the question that keeps nagging at me.

"Mason and those other vampires," I say, "why would they want to do that? If Nepheras and her kind take back the realm, the vampires would serve them. Or did I miss something?"

Beatrice settles back in her chair, letting out a weary sigh. "No, you understand correctly. This has been an ongoing debate for a long time within the vampire community. There's always been a faction believing that they've reached the end of their evolutionary development. That the rise of humankind, especially with the protection of witches, has driven them into the shadows for good. Some vampires feel it's only a matter of time until they're wiped out entirely."

Now, it starts to make sense. "So, they feel it's worth the gamble. Basically, take their chances."

"Essentially," Beatrice says. "It would mean not only an unlimited food source, but nearly infinite opportunities to increase their population. As it is now, if vampires became too noticeable, humans would go to war against them. There was a time when the humans might have lost, but now that seems highly unlikely. Regardless, it's considered a heretical point of view by most vampires. Obviously, there'd be no going back from such a shift."

"Yeah, no kidding. Although I guess whoever's at the top might stand to gain quite a bit. In fact, that vampire might become something like a general in the demon army."

"Which brings us to our friend, Mason. Now you've seen him, you've heard him, and you understand his motivation. But that really doesn't get us any closer to mitigating the threat. The fact is, he can inspire his followers all he wants but it wouldn't make any difference. Not without the element allowing the threat to exist in the first place."

The same goes for Nepheras and Vintain, if I'm not just crazy and he's somehow involved. The existence of that same threat allowed Sarah Wellingsford to cast suspicion upon my sister. "We need to find that veil witch," I say.

Beatrice nods, keeping her eyes on mine. "Yes, we do. I'm assuming he wasn't involved last night or you would have told me."

"Still no sign of him."

So far, we don't even have a name, never mind an understanding of why he's doing what he's doing. Maybe if we just had a clue about who he is, we might be able to understand his motivation. Then, suddenly, something occurs to me. Who do I know that can pluck a name out of thin air, as well as access the thoughts and feelings of someone she's never met?

Beatrice frowns, watching me. "What is it?"

Still, I hesitate. I told myself I'd never involve Julia again, that my doing so before nearly got her killed. Maybe worse than killed.

Beatrice perches forward. "Cassie, this is too important. The stakes are just too high. For all of us, witches and humans alike. If the demons carry out their plan, it would be nothing short of an apocalypse."

I know she's right. There's just no denying it. So I tell her the move I think we should take next, even as I hate myself for doing so.

CHAPTER 18

It's a little after ten when we arrive at the house where Nora used to live, four of us riding in Beatrice's car. Well, at least a car she chose to use tonight. For all I know, the car might belong to the Shadow Order. Or, Beatrice has expensive taste, given that it's a brand new Lexus. But I see now why she suggested we take it, since my car would have stood out like a sore thumb in a neighborhood like this. It never occurred to me that Nora might have lived in a house like the one we're about to enter. I got the impression she'd been comfortable, but not this comfortable.

As if reading my thoughts, Nora turns to me from where she sits beside Beatrice up front. "It's not really as big as it looks."

Yeah, right. The house may not exactly qualify as a mansion, but it's pretty damned big. It looks to be old too, but old in the sense that it was constructed long ago by someone with exquisite taste and plenty of money. In other words, it's a historic home sitting on a large lot that, even at night, I can tell has been kept meticulously groomed.

Julia gazes out from where she sits beside me. "Who owns it? And why are the lights on? I thought…" She doesn't finish her sentence, since obviously she was about to remark on everyone else who lived there being dead. After a moment, she says, "I'm sorry. I'm just curious."

"It's okay," Nora says. "It was owned by Thomas, one of my friends. For the last ten years or so, but we weren't going to be able to stay much longer. "

By which she means that vampires can't stay in the same place for very long. Even if they only come and go at night, someone is bound to notice that they don't age. Clearly, Thomas had money, but that's often the case for beings who are essentially immortal. Even a reasonably substantial inheritance can be turned into a fortune, given enough time and wise investing.

Beatrice kills the engine. "After the arch vampire sent a team to investigate, one of our Shadow Order members agreed to keep up appearances. He's made sure to leave some lights on. He also arranged for cars to come and go at night, since that's usually the case."

It surprises me that she's this open with Julia, but I guess she figures if Julia is willing to take the risk, then she deserves honest answers. Julia's my friend, after all, and embarking on this experiment required that I tell Beatrice about who Julia is to me.

Julia speaks softly, her voice distant. "Is his name Ellis?"

Beatrice tilts her head; she seems surprised at the question. "Yes, Ellis."

"He's one of the Vamanec P'yrin, isn't he?"

Beatrice glances at me. I shake my head to indicate that I didn't tell Julia about him.

"Yes, he is," Beatrice says.

"It bothers him, what happened here," Julia says. "He feels both sad and concerned. Has he been in this car before?"

Beatrice's eyebrows quirk, I suspect involuntarily. "The night before last."

Julia nods, then turns her attention back to the house. After a moment, she says, "We should go in now."

Part of me wants to turn back, to remove Julia from the situation before she gets in any deeper. I understand the stakes. I'd be a fool not to. Still, part of me wants only to protect my friend. We're here, though, aren't we? Which means that it's already too late to change our course of action.

We enter the house through the back, coming into the kitchen. The room is large and spotless, but strangely dated. Except for the refrigerator, all of the appliances look to be decades old. But I guess it makes sense that this room would appear to be rarely used. Until recently, this was a house shared by vampires. They had no need for a kitchen, although it occurs to me why the refrigerator looks new. Stephanie mentioned the possibility of Nora's group having access to a steady supply of blood. Was the refrigerator used to store blood bags? The feeling I get is yes, but I don't really want to know.

As we pass through the room, Nora barely looks around, her manner confirming what I suspected before. This room, the heart of most homes, means little here and must hold few memories.

We pass through a dining room, where notebooks and sketchpads clutter a table alongside brushes and tubes of paint. Several easels are set along one wall, each holding a painting in progress. One depicts a river, sunlight glimmering on the water, another a mountain range at sunrise, hues of gold and rose fanning out across the sky. I glance around but see no photos in this studio, and I imagine that these scenes came from someone's memory. Cherished glimpses of light from a distant time and another life.

We walk up the hall past a sitting room which holds floor-to-ceiling bookshelves, each full to capacity. Many of the books look old, thick leather bound volumes sitting incongruously beside the glossy spines of modern novels. A large desk holds two laptops, one left open. The space of a writer, I think, or at least someone who loved to read.

We pass another room, the family room, and it's all I can do but stop and stare. Not because it's unusual, but just the opposite. There are sofas and chairs, as well as a television mounted to the wall, but it's the photos that make my breath hitch in my throat. They're everywhere, spread across the mantel and hung on the wall. Five people, three men and two women, all of them forever young. The photos show smiling faces at holidays and birthdays, friends with arms thrown across each other's shoulders at clubs and bars. Those photos, of which I catch only a glimpse, show the history of people who've been together for a long time.

We keep walking and I realize that we're following Julia. At some point, we fell in behind her as if in some unspoken accord. She stops as we enter the foyer, to one side the living room and to the other the staircase. She stands quietly, closing her eyes for a moment, and I can tell from her furrowed brow that she's receiving impressions. Then she walks into the living room, waits for us, and sits on the sofa. Her eyes meet mine and she nods.

"You should come," she says.

We didn't discuss it before, but I know she's right. We simply can't risk losing anything she experiences to interpretation. I need to know everything. I need to see and feel what she does.

Still, I can't help but feel apprehensive. Despite all the years I existed within Julia's body, she always kept the psychic part of herself private, just as I too guarded certain memories and emotional experiences. It was only recently that I melded my consciousness with hers to join her in a psychic exploration, an experience I found at first nearly overwhelming in its emotional intensity.

Still, I take a seat beside her, as Beatrice watches us curiously. I have to wonder if, despite all the things she's experienced, this might be new for her. I would imagine it's fairly rare for two women to be able to fuse their minds together.

Nora, on the other hand, seems barely aware of us. She stands by the window with her arms wrapped around herself as if she's cold. I doubt that's the case. I suspect it's difficult for her to be here, in this place where just days ago her friends died. Not just her friends, her family, I think, my mind returning to that room full of photos.

I turn to Julia and speak softly. "Okay, let's do this."

Her eyes meet mine. "Are you sure?"

I force myself not to hesitate. "Yes, I'm sure."

Julia looks from me to where Beatrice stands watching. Then her eyes go to Nora.

Beatrice picks up on what Julia is hesitant to communicate. "Would it be better if we waited elsewhere?"

"It might be," Julia says.

"Of course." Beatrice approaches Nora, gently placing a hand on her shoulder. "Nora, dear," she whispers, "why don't we go talk in the kitchen?"

Without speaking, Nora nods and follows after Beatrice, leaving Julia and me alone. Julia doesn't have to say more; she just closes her eyes and I do the same. I breathe evenly and deeply, invoking the meditative state that will allow me to separate my consciousness from my body. Soon, I sense the glow of Julia's life force beside me, and I imagine myself drifting toward it. In doing so, I return to that place I once thought of as home.

Here I am again.

"Hey there," Julia whispers.

Her voice feels warm and comforting, a soft blanket of affection wrapping itself around me.

I have a feeling this is going to get dark. Are you sure you want to do this?

"Are you?"

Not really.

"Exactly, but we have to. We both know that."

Then I guess it's time for you to unleash your powers, mutant.

Julia laughs at this reminder of our shared joke, that her abilities are more like something out of the X-Men than what comes to mind when most people think of the word "psychic."

"Fasten your seatbelt," Julia whispers.

What happens next starts out quite a bit like last time, as Julia opens her inner senses to the symphony of the collective consciousness. We're soon assailed by a barrage of kaleidoscopic images and feelings all mixed together—a massive psychic wave washing over us, one that would easily carry me off if it wasn't for Julia anchoring me. I hang on, inwardly clenching my eyes as I wait for her to draw in her scope.

Soon, the initial onslaught subsides, darkness and silence settling in around us. That doesn't last long. I jump at a sudden flash of white light and the sight of a man appearing in the foyer of this same room. He looks to be in his twenties, thin and feral with silver hair. He strides toward where another man rises from his chair, a book dropping from his hand. This man is dark and thin, his face a mask of shock. Through Julia, I sense what he felt in this moment—utter disbelief at what he's seeing, anger surging within him, and the desire to protect those around him. This was Thomas, I think, as the other man thrusts out his hand to release a flash of magic. The vampire stumbles back, engulfed in light, already beginning to transform.

He's on his knees, bones showing through his skin, by the time another man appears in the doorway. This one looks young, maybe not much more than a teenager. His eyes go wide and he calls out to the others in his very last act, the veil witch spinning at the sound of his voice. This was William, I think, as he too dies at the hands of the veil witch.

Part of me knows that this scene took place in the past, but that doesn't stop the horror I feel. Just as not having my body doesn't keep my heart from pounding or my tears from falling.

The veil witch leaves the room, where two vampires have been reduced to piles of bones. He starts climbing the stairs as another man appears at the top, like the others young and handsome. He throws himself at his assailant but never makes contact as another strike of magic drives him back. He smashes against the wall and crumples, his skin sloughing off as he rapidly starts to decompose. Joel, I think. This was Joel.

The veil witch reaches the top of the stairs, where he stops and looks down at his kill. He's pleased with himself and the power within him, which keeps growing stronger each day. He stares at the tattoo on his arm, shaped like a serpent and glowing like fire. He whirls around at the sound of a woman's gasp.

She's pale, this one, with long red hair. She's wrapped in a robe like someone preparing for sleep. She turns to flee, but doesn't get far before another magical strike takes her down. This was Emily, I think, as she spills to the ground, her robe pulled up around her bent, white legs.

I can't take anymore. Please, we have to stop!

From what feels like a million miles away, I hear Julia whisper, "We can't. We need to know."

I don't think I can.

"You can," Julia says. "Stay with me."

She's right, of course. Some part of me knows that too, even though I'm not sure how much more I can take.

We shift our vision away from the body, now just bones wrapped in cloth. We watch as the veil witch strides toward where she lays. His grin widens once more. He breathes hard, his nostrils flaring with exhilaration. We lock onto his pale blue eyes, traveling closer and closer, until those eyes loom before us like planets. Then we're inside him.

Images fly backwards at breakneck speed, like a film playing in reverse. First, we see each scene that just played out as we relive the killings. Then we're outside in the moment Nora described, as fiery light shimmers and then grows bright to let two men step through the veil.

We start hurtling backwards again, through a tunnel that flickers and pulses orange, a blur that keeps on going and going while revealing nothing.

I reach out to Julia again. *What is it? Something seems wrong.*

"I don't know," she says. "It's like something's blocking us."

What's blocking us is magic, I'm sure. Someone is keeping us from seeing wherever it is the veil witch went or who he saw there. Which only makes me more determined, every fiber of my being disgusted by those events we witnessed.

Can we move past this part? We'll figure it out later.

"Okay, I'll try."

It only takes a moment, and the tunnel dissolves as images start coming through clear again. We find ourselves in a small apartment. It's spare, the walls blank, the furniture cheap and old. Julia's certainty tells me that this is where he lives. We're getting close, I can feel it. My excitement and determination rises, spurring me on.

Keep going! We can do this!

The scene suddenly changes once more. We're in a building now, an institution of some sort. The walls are made of cinderblock painted light green, the doors lining the hall solid steel. We pass though one of those doors to enter a room where the veil witch sits on a bed, across from him a window secured with thick iron mesh.

Where are we?

A beat, and then Julia says, "I think he lived here."

The light outside the window darkens, then grows brighter, then darkens and brightens again. It happens over and over, as days and then years flicker past, during which the veil witch keeps getting younger and younger. Somehow within me, I know what I'm seeing, but I don't want to face it. Not when I want to feel hate over sympathy. Still, I can't help but think of that woman I never met. My great-grandmother, who was once locked away for being a veil witch.

It feels like we're stuck.

"We are," Julia says. "They kept him here for a long time."

The sense of claustrophobia, the weight of the walls pressing in, becomes all but unbearable. I just can't take any more.

Go forward again. Can we do that?

"Yes, I think so."

Try. We need to know what the connection is.

Suddenly, the vision shifts around us again. We're in Grimoire, where Maggie sits perched behind her counter as the front door opens. The veil witch enters and Maggie looks up, watching him with curious eyes. She's never seen him before, but she knows he's a witch. She can feel the aura of magic around him. We watch as the veil witch approaches her. He knows what to say and which questions to ask. Her reservations drop, her trust building as names are mentioned and connections established. Then they're in back, the veil witch pretending to peruse and Maggie amiably explaining. But it's the image of one book that burns in his mind, along with a name he's just recently learned. As soon as Maggie leaves him to go back out front, he goes to where he's been told he can find it. He removes the book from the shelf to open its pages, the connection becoming clear as Julia burrows deeper and deeper into his mind. Finally, I know who he is and just why he came here.

His name is Silas, and the woman who wrote the book he now holds was his mother.

CHAPTER 19

Isabel answers the door wearing jeans and a flannel shirt, her strawberry-blonde hair tied back in a ponytail. Without makeup and simply dressed, she still looks beautiful. She's just one of those rare women who can seem youthful at fifty. Still, the dark circles beneath her eyes, along with the deepened lines on her forehead, tell a story of worry and sleeplessness. I can only imagine that this must be the longest week of her life.

She opens the door wider to let us in, then gives both me and Autumn a hug. Without hesitation, she hugs Julia too. "It's so nice to meet you," she says. "I've heard so much about you."

Isabel knows my story of course. She's one of the few people to know every detail. Still, it's only now that I realize that these two people, who both mean so much to me, have never met.

"You too," Julia says. "Cassie's told me about all you've done for her."

"As well as me," Autumn says.

Isabel smiles, taking in the three of us. "Well, someone had to clue these two in. You'd think being able to perform magic would have done the trick... "

She lets her words trail off, giving Julia a conspiratorial glance.

"Hey, we didn't know it was magic," I say.

Isabel pretends to frown. "And those orbs you kept lighting up were, what? Your own personal Aurora Borealis?"

I have to laugh, even as my cheeks grow warm. She really does have a point.

"Well, take those jackets off." Isabel says, nodding toward the kitchen. "Come on and I'll get you guys some coffee."

As always, Isabel's kitchen is clean and bright, sunlight gleaming on her hardwood floors. Without even thinking about it, Autumn and I go to the table, so Julia does the same. Isabel brings the coffee, pouring each of us a cup. "Don't be shy," she tells Julia, gesturing to the plate of fruit and cheese she put out for our arrival, along with a loaf of freshly baked bread.

Autumn and I look up with guilty expressions, having already started digging in.

Isabel just laughs. "You better get some before these two eat it all."

She waits until Julia puts a little on her plate, and takes a sip of her coffee. "So Julia," she says, "I've heard about your abilities. What happened last night is extraordinary."

Julia's pale face turns red. "Oh, I don't know," she says. "It's just something I can do."

Isabel raises an eyebrow. "You and maybe two other psychics in the world." She turns to me and adds, "Are you sure this one doesn't have witch blood?"

It's actually a very good question. More and more lately, I've wondered the same. How is it that Julia can take us where we've gone? For that matter, how was she able to host me within her for all those years? My mind returns to last night, and that moment of Beatrice's keen interest. That woman has seen a lot, but I got the feeling she was seeing something new.

Julia's blush deepens at being the center of attention. She tries to laugh it off. "Cassie and I joke about me being a mutant."

Isabel smiles to make her feel comfortable. "But in a way that's what we are. Witches are just humans, but with something extra. Namely, magic. Some speculate that we're an evolutionary offshoot, those whose genes adapted differently. Isn't that what a mutant is?" She gestures to the fruit plate. "Try one of those pears. You'll like those."

She says it as if, before that, she hadn't said anything unusual. But then, I guess she really didn't. She's just talking about witchcraft with other witches. For us, I guess that's normal.

"Where's Phoenix?"

For once, it's Autumn who asks the question, although I was wondering the same thing. Just not for the usual reasons. This time, we came to see Phoenix as a necromancer. We're running out of time and maybe, just maybe, he can help us find the answers we need.

"He should be here soon," Isabel says. "I would imagine any minute."

"He isn't staying here anymore?" I try not to sound overly curious.

Isabel shakes her head. "I made him go home. He has his own life, his animals, his job, and other things to look after. It's not doing him any good thinking he has to keep looking after me."

She tries to sound casual, but I can tell she's hurting. She glances away, and I wonder if, within her mind, she sees that mirror we brought here. Does she check it each night, and every morning, to see if Bethany's image has started to fade? I'm sure she must, at least that often, if not every hour.

I also think of Phoenix, and what Isabel just said. *He has his own life.* It's funny how I think he'll just be here waiting for me, but that's not the way it works. I'd be a fool to think otherwise.

The sound of a truck comes from outside, and Isabel rises from the table. "That must be him now," she says, going to the door.

Phoenix enters the kitchen and gives his mother a hug, focusing only on her as he squeezes her tight. He speaks softly. "Everything okay?"

Isabel nods, for the moment holding onto him. "Yes," she says. "Everything's fine."

It's not, of course, but Isabel is a strong woman—a strong witch. She must cry when she's alone, thinking about her daughter, but she's trying not to burden her son any more than she has to.

Isabel steps back from Phoenix, who turns his attention our way. Like both Isabel and Bethany, he has thick, golden hair, although his eyes are hazel to their green. He smiles at seeing us, but he looks tired, the pain showing in his eyes too. He hangs his jacket on a hook and comes to the table.

"You must be Julia," he says.

"Sorry," I say. "Julia, Phoenix. Phoenix, Julia. Just don't make her blush any more than your mother did."

"I heard that!" Isabel says, from where she's fiddling at the sink. She turns to give me stink-eye.

I have to laugh. "Just saying. We're a socially phobic kind of crowd."

"Kind of true," Autumn says.

"Totally true," Julia says, and then she turns back to Phoenix. "But, hey, I hear you can talk to the dead."

Phoenix shrugs. "On occasion. I hear you can burrow through psychic wormholes."

Sure enough, Julia starts blushing again. "Only in the name of science, and occasionally witchcraft."

Phoenix chuckles and I catch his eye, then nod toward the coffee. "You might want to grab a cup. We have work to do." A little bit bossy. But hey, it's true.

"Yeah, good idea," Phoenix says. "I ran out at my place."

"Wash your hands first," Isabel says. "Especially if you've been touching those dogs of yours."

Her words remind me that some things never change. The entire universe can be about to shatter, but a mother is still a mother.

~~~

Before long, we're getting ready to attempt what we came here to do. It's just Phoenix, Julia and me now, in a room I've never entered before. This room, once intended as a downstairs bedroom, became dedicated years ago as a place for Phoenix to practice necromancy. Needless to say, he too had an unusual childhood.

It's dark inside the room, the curtains drawn closed to the day outside. There's no furniture to speak of, just the rug we sit on and a couple of low tables. One holds rows of gently burning candles, the other a collection of small round vials. On the rug before Phoenix rests a shallow metal basin. It's wide in circumference, at least two feet across, but no more than a few inches deep at its center. I have no idea what it's for, but this kind of magic is as new to me as it is to Julia.

As we sit cross-legged on the floor, I suppose someone seeing us might think we've gathered to meditate. In reality, we're hoping to summon the dead. Well, at least that's what Phoenix will be doing. That ability is the key difference between being a veil witch and a necromancer. While my sister and I often interact with the nonliving, that contact is limited to those who remain in this plane. We're the realm watchers, guardians who can eject those who supernaturally trespass, as well as guides who can free those held trapped here. In a word, psychopomps. Phoenix, on the other hand, can communicate with those holding the keys to the other side, ancient spirits who never took physical form. They live in Death, as the consciousness of that dimension between dimensions.

The reason for Autumn and Isabel not being included is to preserve what Phoenix called the "contact integrity." When communicating with his guides in the realm of spirit, he explained, the memories, thoughts and emotions of those present can affect the outcome. Only Julia and I shared last night's experience, just as it was only us who psychically linked with Lauren Flannery before to break the spell Grayson had cast upon her. For that reason, Phoenix felt that limiting those present would increase our chances for success.

Now, he looks to us, where we sit across from him. "This isn't an experience I often share," he says. "It can be, well, a little weird sometimes."

"Not to mention creepy?" I say.

Phoenix cracks a grin, his eyes cutting to Julia and then back to me. "Basically, yeah. At least until you get used to it. Anyway, let's give it a try and see what happens. Just to warn you, I'm never entirely sure which way it will go."

I think I know what he means. There's no way to be sure if we'll be able to even locate Lauren Flannery's spirit, never mind establish contact. There are just too many variables.

Phoenix takes a deep silent breath, closing his eyes as he centers himself for what's to come. When he feels ready, he opens his eyes again. He reaches for two of the vials. They each hold liquid, what I presume to be potions, one neon blue and the other the color of mercury. Phoenix uncorks them, tipping their contents into opposite sides of the basin. Slowly, they run down toward the center and start to swirl in a spiral, somehow not mixing. A light vapor starts to rise, smoky tendrils twisting into the air.

Phoenix seems not to notice as he once again closes his eyes. He begins to recite an incantation, his voice barely audible as he speaks in what sounds like Latin or some other dead language. A sudden chill of recognition ripples through me. From where or when, I'm not sure, but I get the feeling I once spoke this language too. Along with that feeling come images. I see a village with stone cottages and ox-drawn carts traveling on paths of dirt. What am I seeing?

The vision dissipates as, beside me, Julia takes a quick and sudden breath. I look to see her widened eyes, and then track her gaze to Phoenix's hands, which have begun to glow. I double-check to be sure, but there's no doubt that Julia sees what's happening. Which makes me wonder once more. While non-magical humans can feel the effects of witch magic, I've never known one to see its source. Until now, I've always assumed it was that way for Julia.

The basin flares with a sudden whoosh, drawing my attention back again. The vapors, gently rising as tendrils before, now thicken into a twisting column, one that soon takes on spectral form. It's tall, shaped like a person and nearly reaching the ceiling. It has a head but no face, and limbs but no hands. Instinctively, I know it needs neither eyes to see, a mouth to speak, nor hands to feel. What I'm seeing is pure spirit. An energy without any ties to physicality.

I cut a quick glance over at Julia to confirm that she sees it too. Her eyes are even wider now, her mouth having dropped open as she stares. My gaze goes back to the figure, which turns slowly, as if looking around the room. My entire body thrums with the magic surging around me, as if every nerve ending has lit up from the sudden shift in energy.

Phoenix slowly raises his face. In a quiet voice, he addresses the being he summoned. "The one in her last life called Lauren Flannery. Do you feel her connected to us?"

The column of vapor twists, the human shape all but disappearing before taking form again. It tilts its head down, first at Julia and then at me. Then the spirit twists around to face Phoenix again.

I hear nothing, but apparently it's not the same for Phoenix. "Yes, both of them," he says. "Together both times."

Again, he hears words that I can't as the spirit speaks to him.

"That's right, she came to the one called Cassie first. She needed help."

Moments pass, Phoenix appearing to listen, this time as the spirit bends in low over him. I almost jump up, but then restrain myself, as it lowers vaporous limbs to plant them on either side of Phoenix's head.

Phoenix speaks softly. "You have my permission."

Despite all the magic I've seen, I'm not quite ready for what happens next. The spirit turns within the basin, bending now to look down just at me. At the same time, Phoenix's eyes roll up into his head. His mouth opens, and one word comes out in a voice that's low and hoarse. "Ask."

That's it and no more as the spirit waits for a response. Apparently, the floor is mine.

"We'd like to speak to Lauren Flannery," I say. "I don't exactly know her, but she came to me. First, as a ghost, but then through her Book of Shadows."

The blue smoke of the spirit's body twists and swirls. I wait for an answer, but one doesn't come. Then I realize why. Because I was rambling. I didn't ask a question.

I try again. "Can we speak to her?"

Again, I get nothing. Right, literal, I think. It's not talking to *us*, it's talking to *me*.

"Can *I* speak to her?"

The vaporous column slowly shakes its head. "No."

Okay, I think I've got this. No nuance. Just direct questions. "Why?"

"She is in the healing realm. She cannot be summoned here."

Damn. The length of that response leaves me stunned. That was downright chatty for... What is this thing, exactly? I guess Phoenix would call it a guide, although I always pictured something different. But this isn't good. The entire point was making contact with Lauren Flannery, in the hope that we might learn more about Silas.

I snap out of it when the strange voice comes through Phoenix again. "Do you have more questions?"

I get the feeling it's losing patience. I look to Phoenix for advice, which makes no sense. He remains, well, possessed. I'm not sure what else to call it.

Then I have an idea. If the spirit can speak through Phoenix…

I shift my attention back to the guide. "Can she speak to me through you?" Then, to be sure I'm covering all the angles I add, "Or can you ask her questions?"

My heartbeat kicks up a notch when the guide says, "I can ask her questions."

Just to be absolutely sure, I say, "Can you tell me what she says?"

"Yes."

Well, why didn't you just say so before, you big chimney? Because, I didn't ask, of course.

Come on, Cassie. Think! Get to what you need to know.

"Did she have a son?" Technically, I already know this, but I'm not sure how best to proceed.

A few moments pass. "Yes."

"Did she raise him?"

It's just a gut feeling, but we saw only places. We never saw any connection between Silas and other people.

"She did not," the guide says.

It's like pulling teeth, but we've gotten this far. I'm not giving up now. "Why not?"

Another pause, and then the spirit says, "She put the child up for adoption."

162

Okay, now we're getting somewhere. "How old was she when she had him?"

"Seventeen." That time there was almost no pause, making me wonder if the connection to Lauren is getting stronger. Or if there's some sense of urgency on her part to convey the information.

"Who knew about the child?"

"There were two, those who were her parents at the time."

Shit. So, I guess that's it. Lauren didn't raise Silas, and only her parents knew about his birth. Apparently, I've been barking up the wrong tree, which means we've just wasted our time.

Then the guide says, "There was one other."

A chill ripples down my spine. If it was anyone but Lauren Flannery, I'd tell myself that it can't be who I think. I'd tell myself I'm just paranoid, that I have to stop trying to connect him to what's been happening. As I bring my attention back to the guide, I feel like a tunnel is closing in around me. Still, I have to ask. "Who was that person?"

A pause follows as I dig my nails into my palms.

Then the guide says, "In your plane, Lauren Flannery knew him as Grayson. "

CHAPTER 20

Our necromancy session ended not long after the creepy spirit guide dropped that bomb about Grayson. That was as far as we got before it communicated to Phoenix that it had to leave. Apparently, it had places to go and dead people to meet. Or maybe it was just getting bored. I don't know, because it didn't offer an explanation. Then it was gone and we were on our own again. Frankly, it came as a relief. After that, we shared what we knew with Autumn and Isabel. After hours of group speculation, this is the scenario we came up with:

Lauren never knew her son, nor did she name him. The name, Silas, must have been bestowed upon him by a nurse or orphanage administrator. He must never have been adopted, and at some point ended up institutionalized for suffering from delusions. Although, of course, those weren't delusions. Silas was coming into his magic.

As for Lauren Flannery, we already knew that she later fell in love with Grayson. Apparently, she decided there shouldn't be any secrets between them. So, she confided in him about the baby she'd once given up for adoption. Presumably, Grayson hadn't seemed concerned with her past.

Of course, Grayson wasn't really Grayson. He was Vintain, to whom that kind of information was like striking gold. At some point, he must have tracked Silas down. How, we have no idea, but presumably by means of magic. After all, he was a mage, one whose primary mission had become tracking down veil witches. From there, we guessed he must have become involved in Silas's life. To what extent, we just couldn't say. But we supposed it didn't really matter, other than the fact that some sort of connection was established.

As for what Silas told Maggie—that he'd met Vintain while traveling—who can say what that really meant? Cryptic, to say the least. The way we figured it, he probably just used that as a ploy to gain her trust. It worked, apparently, since he ended up with his mother's Book of Shadows. Why he wanted it is unclear. Sentimentality, or simple curiosity; both occurred to us. Then again, that book might have been just a loose end that Vintain wanted gone. After all, it offered proof that he'd recently appeared here as a changeling. Why leave that lying around if he didn't have to?

Were we wrong about anything? Probably yes, but that was the best we could come up with. And it definitely didn't hurt to have a psychic in the room.

By the time we're done talking, it's almost two. We're finishing the lunch Isabel insists on providing before we drive back. Still, two questions linger. Have we gotten any closer to saving Bethany, or to proving Autumn innocent? The fact is, I think so, in that at least we know what we're up against. Well, technically, what I'm up against. I realize it's their fight too, but right now Autumn has no magic and

I'm just not sure about bringing the others to Faerie, which is where I need to go next. I suspect I could bring them, now that Seelie no longer control the magic. I'm just not sure it's a good idea. At least, not until we know more.

I'm just finishing helping with the dishes, when Phoenix comes up beside me at the sink. He nods toward the back door and speaks softly. "Got time to take a walk?"

Our eyes meet and I can see that he wants to talk. I dry my hands and turn to where Isabel, Autumn and Julia hover at the table. "Guys, we'll be back in a bit," I say.

Soon, Phoenix and I stroll past the barns and onto a path leading toward the orchard. The afternoon sun shines through the leafless branches of apple, pear and cherry trees.

"So, I've been thinking," Phoenix says.

I expect him to add more, but he doesn't. "Yeah?"

He chuckles. "Sorry. Not sure how to phrase it exactly, but I'm thinking, either way, we're going to be in each other's lives."

I'd definitely like him to add more there too, but he leaves me hanging again. I give him a soft nudge with my elbow. "It does seem to keep going that way."

He cracks a grin. "Exactly. I guess what I'm saying is, I'm not sure what the future is going to bring. We need to get past this part first."

He's totally right, of course. At one point, I didn't doubt we had a future together. That still might be, but for now everything is on hold. "True enough," I say. "So what's on your mind?"

He glances over at me, his eyes meeting mine as we continue walking. "That maybe I should tell you what happened. Unless you don't care, of course."

I know immediately what he means. And, yes, I still care. "I've kind of wondered a few times," I admit. As in I obsessed over it for a while, the image of him kissing that girl somehow burned onto my retina.

"So, here's the deal," Phoenix says. "When you said you needed some time, I wasn't worried about it. At least, I understood. You'd been through a lot, and I figured you needed to process things."

"That's true, I did," I say, and it really is the truth. So much had happened so fast that I could barely think.

"But then you stopped calling, or answering texts. So, I figured I should probably move on."

I stopped answering texts? Wow, that's just not okay. "Sorry," I say. "I was sort of going through a strange time."

Then again, when am I not?

Phoenix shrugs. "I know. You were just moving into your new place and you'd never really been on your own before. You went from being a kid, to living inside Julia's body, to suddenly being an adult living at your mother's house. You needed time to think. I get that."

What's funny is that I never told him any of that. He just somehow knew what I was going through. "Sorry," I say again.

"Don't be," Phoenix says. "That's not what this is about. But I'm not going to lie. I was trying to forget you, since I figured that had to happen. And that's when

Theresa called." Before I can ask, he adds, "An old girlfriend. She lives up north now, but her family is still here. Anyway, she was someone I used to care for. I still do. Just not like that, as it turns out."

I turn to search his face. "Was that the moment I saw?"

Phoenix nods. "Yeah. To be honest, I was hoping I'd feel differently, but I knew as soon as we kissed. Of course, it probably didn't help that you were driving by staring at us."

A grin spreads across his face and I have to laugh. Phoenix laughs too.

"Looking back, I probably should have called first," I say.

"Don't worry about it. It wasn't going to work out anyway. You being there just kind of hammered the point home."

We're past the orchard, approaching a creek that cuts through the property. Light glimmers off the rippling water. For a few moments, we walk in silence.

Then Phoenix says, "Anyway, I figured I should probably tell you."

"Thanks," I say softly.

What's strange is that, before, I felt like the wronged party, but it doesn't look that way now. I may not have exactly broken up with Phoenix, but I definitely left him hanging. Then I went on to have a relationship with Esras. Was I just trying to forget about seeing Phoenix with that girl? At the time, maybe, but it runs deeper than that, I know. I got scared and I ran. Then I did it again.

I figure it's cards on the table time. After all, Phoenix came clean with me.

"I sort of met someone," I say.

Phoenix just nods. "I kind of figured. Was it in Faerie?"

And there I was thinking I'm hard to read, a girl full of mystery and secrets, when it's probably been written all over my face. "Yes," I say. "But I don't think it could work out."

"Do you love him?"

The question takes me by surprise, partly because of the way he asks. There's no anger in his voice, or resentment. It's just an honest question between friends.

So I give him an honest answer. "I'm not sure."

And maybe the rest goes without saying, but it's there all the same, because I didn't say no. Somehow, I know that Phoenix gets it. The fact is, I love them both, but I'm not sure either can happen. Not until I figure out who I am. And if I never do?

Phoenix reaches for my hand just like he used to, without demand or expectation. Just an offer of comfort. So I wrap my hand around his, as a cool breeze blows past and the sun paints the fields with golden light.

"Love makes witchcraft seem simple," Phoenix says.

I sigh and lean into him, touching my head to his shoulder. Then we keep walking, both of us sad and still holding onto each other.

CHAPTER 21

Cade and I stride down the cobblestone street toward the palace, once home to High Queen Abarrane and her High Mage Vintain, now inhabited by Faerie's interim leaders, Esras and Revlen. Thanks to the time difference between the two realms, it's late afternoon here when it was evening back home. It's also spring to our winter, the sun fairly high in the sky. That's part of why I decided to come right away, rather than wait until morning. That and the fact that I couldn't have possibly slept.

Cade, on the other hand wasn't nearly as eager. In fact, his pub was full when I showed up out of nowhere to yank him out of there. The result being that he's been grumbling the entire time we've been walking.

That grumbling continues as we approach the main gates. "We should have sent a messenger first. What if they're not here?"

"They run this place now. Where else would they be?"

My half-baked logic doesn't quite work for Cade. "This is crazy," he says. "Vintain is in prison. Which you know, because you helped put him there."

It's not the first time he's made this point and, of course, he's right. I have no idea how Vintain is influencing Silas's actions, but I know that he is somehow. Without Vintain being involved, nothing Silas has done makes any sense. On the other hand, factor Vintain into the picture and things start to connect. Maybe not all of them, but it definitely explains why a veil witch we never met before would suddenly come after us. This is at least partly personal, which is what we've strongly suspected from the moment Bethany went missing.

"I never said he wasn't in prison," I repeat for at least the fifth time. "I just said he's part of it."

Cade sighs, puffing to keep up with me. I guess those vampire workouts must be paying off. "You can see where I might find that a little confusing."

"Good to know I'm not alone."

Reaching the gates, we stop walking, although I'm surprised to see them open.

Cade notices my puzzled expression. "Yeah, that part's been changed. Sort of a symbolic gesture, now that there's no threat to the realm."

"That's nice," I say, and it is nice that the people of Faerie no longer feel cut off from their leaders. At that same time, I can't get past the feeling that the realm isn't yet out of danger.

We watch as one of the guards rides up on her horse. She's a big woman, with a hawk perched on one of her shoulders. Gone is the uniform of the Royal Guard. She wears a plain tunic, leather leggings and high boots. She doesn't reach for her sword as she brings her horse to a stop before us. "Hello, friends," she says. "How can I help you?"

"We came to speak with Esras and Revlen," Cade says.

Her gaze shifts from me to Cade and then back to me. Her eyes widen with recognition. "Of course," she says. "I'll tell them that Cassie the Fae Witch has arrived." She shakes her head, as if to get over her shock at seeing me, then turns her attention back to Cade. "And you are?"

Cade frowns, planting his hands on his hips. "I'm *Cade*," he says. "I fought for the rebel cause."

The guard tilts her head, as if trying to place his face. Apparently, that doesn't happen. "Of course, sir. Cade, is it?"

Cade speaks through gritted teeth. "Yes, Cade."

I cover my mouth, trying to stifle a laugh, as the guard whispers to her hawk. Then the hawk looks directly at me and caws out, "Cassie the Fae Witch!"

I stare back, shocked, until I make the connection. It must be lingualawk. Right, it's time to recalibrate. I'm back in Faerie again.

The bird swivels its head toward Cade. "Name?"

The guard whispers to her hawk again. "Cade, apparently."

"Cade?" the hawk says.

"Yes, Cade," the guard whispers. "Now go."

The hawk launches off her shoulder and shoots through the air toward the upper level of the palace, where it disappears behind the ornate roofline. Damn, those birds are cool, but these guys really should put in some cell towers.

The guard turns to me again. "It shouldn't be more than a few minutes."

Meanwhile, Cade shuffles and mutters under his breath. "Geez, I was only the guy who snuck us into the palace to begin with."

I pat him on the shoulder and speak softly. "Yes, you did."

"The freaking *hawk* didn't even recognize me."

"It's just a bird," I whisper, trying to make him feel better.

"Lingualawks often test at an IQ score over one-twenty," Cade says.

"Oh." I try not to laugh, but can't stop it from bubbling up inside me.

"Shut up," Cade says, which seals the deal. I stare at the ground, my shoulders convulsing.

"Not funny," Cade says.

I snort again, refusing to look at him.

"I'm going to get you for this," Cade whispers, guaranteeing that I lose my shit.

I keep laughing and staring down until I hear the guard's voice again.

"Please follow me."

In the moments that passed, she dismounted from her horse, which trots off as if it knows exactly where it's going. Of course it does. On top of that, the lingualawk is already back on her shoulder. Wow, that was fast. There I was thinking they'd be better off texting.

As we follow the guard toward the doors of the palace, I do my best to think happy thoughts. I try to concentrate on memories of Cade and Dabria's wedding, which marked the last time I came here. Still, this place evokes much darker memories for me. Memories that insist on making themselves known. I remember Cade and I thinking we'd rescued Ellie Kaminski, only to end up captured. I remember waking up from Vintain's spell to find myself sitting across from him, his ice cold eyes staring into mine. I relive refusing to help him, and how Queen Abarrane used her magic to string me up like a puppet. She flayed my consciousness as she bored into the deepest recesses of my mind, searching for the incantation she'd sought for so long. My pulse starts to escalate, sweat building on my brow, while the world feels like it's closing in around me.

Then the palace doors swing inward, opened by two more guards, and my anxieties dissipate. Esras stands in the foyer, his eyes meeting mine as a smile spreads across his lips. Poised and regal as always, he acknowledges both of us. "Well, to what do I owe this pleasure?"

Cade gestures my way. "Her," he says in a grumpy tone.

Okay, so the damned bird didn't recognize him. "Get over it," I say.

Cade ignores me, speaking to Esras instead. "You might want to talk to your guard. She had no idea who I am."

Esras's cheeks flush a little, as he points to a spot on the wall holding a row of paintings. "Yours is coming soon, I promise."

Oh, great. He means well, but that only makes things worse. The wall holds portraits of those who fought to bring down the Seelie regime. Esras included, of course, along with Revlen and her right-hand men. I'm there too, with a blank space beside me, presumably meant for Cade.

Cade raises his eyebrows in disbelief. "Seriously?"

"By next month, I promise," Esras says. "The painter had to take a week off."

Okay, skip the cell towers guys. But at least get a camera?

"We need to talk," I say.

Esras's eyes return to mine. "I assumed so. Please."

He gestures to a winding staircase and we follow him up to find Revlen waiting on the landing. Like Esras and the guard, she too keeps a sword at her hip. I think of something Esras and I once discussed, how at one time the battles of Faerie were fought with magic. Then that magic came to be possessed by just the few, who in the end were defeated when that magic escaped them. I suspect it will be a while before those of Faerie rely on magic as their primary defense, if in fact they ever do again.

Revlen regards us with her one golden eye, a black eyepatch covering the one she lost. "This way," she says.

Down to business, as always. Revlen is not a woman to mess around. As a group, we follow her down the hall and through a set of doors to enter a meeting room. It's an expansive space, with tapestries upon the walls and tall arched windows, but its function is made evident by the fact it holds just one long table surrounded by chairs. Revlen takes a seat and we do the same, the four of us grouped at the tip of a table meant to accommodate many more.

175

"What's going on?" Revlen says.

Since she's getting right to the point, I do the same. "Vintain," I say. "That's what's going on."

Revlen shakes her head, her eyes cutting to Esras before returning to mine. "I don't understand."

She thinks I'm crazy, I can tell, and I don't blame her. "Neither do I," I say, "but that's why I'm here. Bad things keep happening and he has something to do with it."

Understandably, an awkward silence follows. I expected about the same.

On the surface, my claim seems ridiculous, but I already know that. So, I plow forth anyway. I tell them about how my magic first failed me at Martha Sanders' house, and how we soon discovered that mirror holding Bethany's image. I tell them about the demon activity, the missing witches, the hostile coven meeting, and the magical forces I went up against to save Wendy. I tell them about the murdered vampires, the accusation upon my sister, working with Nora and how we witnessed the Shared Feast. And, of course, I tell them about Silas, as I place the cherry on top of my nightmare sundae.

"Take one guess who else knows about our new veil witch friend," I say.

I see in their expressions that they know the answer. Still, no one wants to be the first to say it.

So, I say it for them. "Right, Vintain. Well, at least Vintain when he was Grayson. Who not only knew Silas's mother, but cast a spell upon her when she could have blown his cover."

"Shit," Cade says, his eyes going wide.

"Right, exactly," I say. "A great big pile of it, and now I'm holding the shovel."

The expressions on Revlen's and Esras's faces have shifted too. They still look confused, but less convinced that I'm crazy. Any way you slice and dice it, there's just no way to ignore the coincidence.

And then we end up right back where we started. "But it makes no sense," Revlen says, keeping her gaze squarely on mine. "Vintain is locked up."

"His trial starts next month," Esras says. "At which point the people of Faerie will decide his fate."

"Well, when was the last time you guys talked to him?"

Esras and Revlen both frown.

"He's under constant guard at Griffin Heights," Revlen says.

"Griffin Heights? Sounds like a country club." I picture Vintain sipping tea while reading a newspaper. Wait, this is Faerie. Someone probably recites the news from a scroll.

Revlen narrows her eyes. "In eight-hundred years, no one has ever escaped."

Okay, I have to admit that's an impressive track record. But still, we're talking about Vintain. "We need to go there," I say.

Esras raises his eyebrows. "Cassie, I assure you—"

I grit my teeth and say it again. "We need to go there. We need to do it now."

~~~

I'm not sure if it's because they decided to take me seriously, or if it's just to humor me, but we ride out right after our meeting. I haven't been on horseback since the last time I was here, but that part isn't a problem. I'd like to think it comes back naturally—kind of like riding a bike—but it's more about the horse than me. For one thing, horses in Faerie are smarter than most people I know. On top of that, I'm riding the same horse. Andor, who, of course, remembers me. Yes, I remember him too, from when he decided to hedge his bets by following centaur orders. Then again, it's hard to stay mad at him. They were horse-people, after all. Well, that and I kind of forgot that he might need food or water. So, sue me. I'm a city girl.

The ride is longer than I expected, the prison nearly an hour outside of Scintillia, but I might be enjoying it if not for the edginess simmering in my core. That and my ass is killing me. I could swear Andor keeps the ride rough on purpose. Still, every time I call him out on it, he just turns and bats long lashes against big brown eyes. Faker.

As the prison comes into view, I see how Griffin Heights got its name. Looming figures perched at intervals atop the tall stone walls, that at first I take to be gargoyles, are actually living creatures watching our approach. Every so often one of them moves, tilting its eagle head or flexing massive wings attached to a lion's body. They are, of course, griffins.

"Damn, and I thought the centaurs were creepy," I say, glancing over at Esras who rides beside me. "Are there any mythological creatures you guys don't have here?"

"They're only mythological in your realm," Revlen says, turning from where she rides in front next to Cade. "But to answer your question, we don't have octopus or gorillas."

"But those aren't—" I stop speaking, her point sinking in. "Wait, you guys don't have octopus?" *Is that supposed to be octopi? I can never remember.*

She shudders. "They're terrifying to even think about."

Geez, what's terrifying about a giant creature with tentacles lurking beneath the water? My gaze goes to the griffins again as two of them take to the air. One circles a row of towers, while the other flies in low over the prison yard. "Are they doing what I think they're doing?"

"Their vigilance is unparalleled," Esras informs me. "Which is part of why no one has ever escaped."

I know he's trying to make me feel better, but it doesn't quite work. "Are they the only guards?"

All three of my fellow riders turn to look at me, and I get it. I'm sure not much gets past the watchful gaze of flying eagle-cats with wings. At the same time, they're just animals. Well, Faerie animals, so they're probably members of Mensa. But still.

Finally, Revlen says, "There are fae guards as well, of course. Vintain has a detail assigned specifically to him, as does—" she catches herself before saying Queen— "Prisoner Abarrane."

Right, she's definitely not queen anymore. Would that make her Lady Abarrane? Not that Revlen is likely to use that title either.

Bells ring as we make our approach, our arrival expected because of a lingualawk Esras dispatched earlier. Nonetheless, more griffins lift to the air, circling as two monolithic steel gates swing inward to let us through. I can't help but nervously glance up, my attention drawn by swishing tails, giant hooked beaks and razor sharp talons.

I ask quietly, "How do they know who we are?"

"They don't," Esras says. "They'll kill anyone they're ordered to kill."

Comforting.

"They also eat them after," he adds.

"Thanks for letting me know."

As we enter the prison grounds, guards stand lined at attention along the walkway. Each guard is tall and broad-shouldered, wearing the same uniform of leather leggings and tunic. Each wears a baldric across his chest to support the sword at his hip. Many are of darker complexion, their hair brown and black. Others are pale and blonde, their irises hues of purple, sea green and orange.

I keep my voice low so that only Esras can hear. "There are Seelie guards?"

He nods toward the men we pass, speaking softly back to me. "Of course."

"But they're Seelie."

Esras turns so that his eyes meet mine. "So am I."

He's right, of course. Not all Seelies have a pale complexion and those otherworldly eyes. Just enough to consistently give me the creeps. Still, I never should have said it. "That's not what I mean," I say, trying to recover. "How do you know they're not loyalists?"

"The loyalists fled," Esras says. "You know that, Cassie. Thousands of them. Other than those who were caught, of course."

My gut twists even more, since Esras's father, mother and brother were among those apprehended. I can't help but wonder if they might even be in this same prison. I hope not, or I'd hate myself for making him come here. I can't imagine the pain he must feel, despite having been at odds with them for decades.

I resist the urge to reach for his hand. "I'm sorry."

"Don't be," Esras says, the warmth returning to his voice. "You're just trying to help your sister. Besides, I should have explained that all of the guards are new. To be on the safe side, those assigned here before were given new posts. There weren't very many remaining."

I feel a little better at hearing that, since hopefully the guards assigned here now have all been sufficiently vetted. Presumably, it's safe to assume that none of the griffins were loyalists.

We soon reach another wall, lower this time, but still at least twenty feet tall. We're escorted through more steel gates by a guard who'd been waiting to meet us.

"Keveris, how are you?" Revlen says, stopping to extend her hand. Clearly, these two know each other, since Keveris smiles warmly at seeing her. He's barrel-chested and brawny, with curly dark hair. Almost certainly Unseelie, which Revlen confirms. "Keveris served the rebel cause bravely. He's in charge of the guards here these days." She turns her attention back to Keveris. "Thank you for your continued service."

"Of course, Commander," he says. "Right this way, please."

We soon reach another wall with another gate, while above us two griffins keep circling. We enter another yard, yet again enclosed by a wall. The only thing in front of us this time is a tower rising high into the sky. It has be at least two-hundred feet tall.

Cade sidles up beside me. "They call it the Tower of Solitude."

"Is that where…?" I can't quite finish the sentence at the thought of being in Vintain's presence again. Not just because of the vicious things he's done, but because of the way he used me. When he posed as Grayson, I came close to falling in love with him. No wonder I'm messed up. At one point I wanted to bonk the same guy who was hoping to kill me. Another one to add to my therapy list.

"That's where they keep him," Cade says. "Notice anything unusual?"

At first I don't, but then I try to think like Cade, a man who served the rebel cause as a professional burglar. I examine the tower again, observing many small barred windows rising to pointed arches in the usual fae architectural style. Then I realize that the only door is at the very top, one small, gray rectangle of stone.

"How do we get in?"

"Or out," Cade says, arching an eyebrow.

"There must be charms," I say. "Hidden doors."

Cade shakes his head.

"Some sort of tunnel?"

He shakes his head again, saying nothing.

"Are you quizzing me?"

"Evidently," Cade says. "So far you're failing. Look for the obvious answer."

At that same moment, a shadow falls over us. I look up to see those griffins still circling.

"No fucking way."

"You guessed it," Cade says. "Get ready."

CHAPTER 22

At that same moment, Keveris blows hard into a whistle, the shrill noise making me jump. I didn't realize he was standing right next to me, the sneaky bastard. What's with this week and whistles?

Covering my ears in case he does it again, I stare up to make sure I'm not seeing things. As far as I can tell, the griffins have grabbed hold of something with their clawed front feet and they're lifting it out from the side of the tower. No, I'm not seeing things. They're grasping chains attached to a small wooden platform, letting it swing beneath them as they flap their way downward.

Esras tries to reassure me. "It's not as bad as you think. Basically, it's what you'd call an elevator in your realm."

I look up again in the fading light. "On the outside of a building?"

He shrugs. "In this case, yes."

"Powered by griffins?"

He shrugs. "Don't worry. It has railings."

That makes me feel way better. As long as I don't fall off the puny wooden platform being hoisted into the sky by magical creatures, I should be fine. The griffins are still making their way down and my palms are already slick with sweat. But if I understand things correctly, and I'm pretty sure I do, there's no other way in or out of the tower. Great.

I jump as the platform slams to the ground. The griffins hold onto it by chains from above, their wings still flapping away. It's either get in or go home. So, like an idiot, I get in along with everyone else. This involves climbing over metal pipes welded together to form the rails. Definitely glad I'm not wearing a skirt. From there, I drop myself onto what's basically a shallow wooden box. No wonder no one ever escapes from this place. It's just safer to stay inside.

"I have a question," I say, looking up to where the griffins hover above us, presumably waiting for a command.

"Of course," Keveris says.

"Have they ever dropped this thing?"

He looks up too, frowning as he thinks. "Those two? I don't think so."

"Wait, are you saying—?"

I don't finish my question because Keveris blows his whistle right next to my ear. I stumble back, partly because of the pain, and partly because the platform tilts as we leave the ground. I pitch forward again as the griffins attempt to balance their load. My stomach lurches as they start soaring upward, and I grab hold of the rails with sweaty hands. Wonderful. I can barely keep my grip and I start sliding sideways. Didn't anyone train the griffins on the concept of level? Or maybe these two haven't dropped the elevator yet because it's their first day on the job.

Cade grabs onto my arm to steady me, his eyes bright with excitement. "Isn't this amazing?"

Seriously? We're not at Six Flags, we're being yanked through the air on a board. "Yeah, it's fantastic," I mutter, doing my best not to hurl on his shoes. "By the way, couldn't anyone order the griffins to take them up or down? How's that a secure system?"

The platform tilts again, Cade grabbing onto me as I start sliding away. "There's only one whistle, and it's magically calibrated for the head guard. If anyone else blows into it, nothing happens."

I let that sink in for a moment. "So, if something happens to the head guard or the whistle..."

Cade shrugs. "Yeah, I know. It's kind of a dicey setup. By the way, forget about riding a griffin in any other way. Try to touch one of those bastards and they'll bite your arm off."

Well, that sure helps, not that I was thinking of riding a griffin. I close my eyes and hang onto Cade, contemplating just how many prison guards must have died over the years trapped in that tower. Cade had to be making up that part about the magical whistle.

A jolting thump forces me to open my eyes again as the griffins bounce us against stone. Wondering if we're at the top, I make the mistake of looking down. Yeah, that's definitely where we are. From up here, I see the tiny antlike forms of the prison guards patrolling the yards below. My stomach lurches again and I'm all but overwhelmed by a spell of dizziness. This time it's Esras who grabs hold of me, his strong hands embracing my midsection.

"Are you okay?"

I look into his eyes as the dizziness subsides. Then I start to feel something else. Oh no, this can't really be happening. Not up here, and not right now. But I can't deny it as a wave of pleasure runs through me. A warm vibration ripples up my ribcage and across my chest, as well as down to, well...

I step out of his embrace, feeling the heat rise to my face. "I'm fine now, thanks."

Esras's eyes linger on mine, but his expression remains only one of concern. Does he really not know? He has to, right?

"Okay, here we are."

I snap out of it at the sound of Keveris's voice, and then I turn to see that the door I spotted from below has swung open. Another guard stands inside waiting for us to enter. I guess when the griffins bashed us into the side of the tower, that was their way of knocking. Then I notice that Keveris has opened a gate to let us get off. There was a gate? Why the hell did we climb over the rails?

Keveris gestures toward the tower door. "Watch your step, now."

Talk about an understatement. He says it casually, like we're about to climb onto an escalator. Meanwhile, the platform still wobbles as the griffins flap their wings above us. There's also at least a two-foot gap between the platform and the door. Slipping through means plunging to your death. And my imagination, always my best friend, ponders whether griffins eat all dead people or just those they kill. I really can't wait to do this again. If it wasn't for the Esras-induced wave of horniness relieving me of my vertigo, there's no doubt I'd completely freak out. As it is, I'm still pretty shaky.

"Watch me," Revlen says. "I'll go first."

Of course she'll go first. She's as gutsy as they come. She steps off the vibrating platform and into the tower like it's nothing. Which, to her, I guess it is. She's been staring death in the face since she was ten.

"Okay, who's next?" Keveris says.

Do I catch a note of impatience in his voice? I could swear I do, but Cade nimbly hops over the gap. Showoff. But he's had years of scaling the sides of buildings as part of his burglar routine to prepare for this moment.

Wait, can I levitate? Actually, no. Not because I don't have magic—I'm sure I do—but because there's no way I'm taking that risk. That would just be idiotic.

"Here, let me help you," Esras says, holding his hand out.

Normally, I wouldn't think of relying on a man for courage—and I don't this time either—but I figure a euphoric boost can't hurt.

I step in front of him, and then look back over my shoulder. "Sure, if you could just…"

Esras grips me on both sides of my midriff. "I've got you," he says.

Oh, yes he does. Damn. In fact, I hate to leave, but I take advantage of his fear-numbing touch to leap through the door like a mountain goat.

Cade's eyes go wide from where he waits beside Revlen inside. "Nice," he says. "I thought you were scared."

I shake my head. "Scared? Nah. Just distracted."

"Right behind you," Esras says, touching me on the shoulder. I briefly think about arching back into him, but I might knock him out of the tower.

Then the door slams closed behind us, plunging us into darkness. That must be one thick door, because I just barely hear Keveris blow his whistle on the other side, commanding the griffins to take him down. So, at least that part goes well.

As my eyes adjust, I see that we stand within a torchlit chamber. It has two doors, each on opposite walls. Beside one of them, a guard stands waiting. He's thin and fair, with dark violet eyes. Presumably, Seelie. He regards us with a serious expression, nodding first to Esras and then Revlen in recognition of their status.

"I'm Loctulan," he says. "I've been asked to escort you to the prisoner's cell. Please follow me."

With that, he turns and starts walking, guiding us down a narrow hall. The walls hold torches lighting our way, their flames reminding me that the Seelie used to light their rooms with magic. Which brings to mind something I've been meaning to dig into a little deeper.

I turn to Revlen, who walks beside me. "You said Vintain remains without access to magic. How can you be sure?"

Revlen keeps striding forward, her posture that of a soldier. "For several reasons. First, because you destroyed the Amulus he was using to monopolize power. Second, because you removed any remaining magic from him when the ley line shared her power with you. Third, because when you left this realm—breaking the spell you'd placed upon him—Vintain had already been placed within his cell, which is surrounded by powerful wards calibrated specifically for him."

"How does that work?"

"By using what you would call a person's DNA."

I raise my eyebrows, taken aback. "Blood magic?"

Revlen shrugs. "What we Unseelie call Vrathax. But, yes, it's essentially what a human witch would call blood magic."

The fae using blood magic never occurred to me, but in this case I have no problem with it. I also have no doubt that the ley line would never entrust her magic to Vintain again. In this realm, she's a sentient being, and there's no way she'd forget the man who once held her in chains. Still, why do I get the feeling that something didn't hold?

We come to another door and wait as Loctulan selects a key from a ring. "There are only two prisoners kept in this tower," he explains. "One on this side and one on the other."

"Is that Abarrane?" I say.

He nods and inserts the key into the lock. "Yes, although they never have contact with each other. For anyone being kept up here, they might as well be the last man on Faerie."

It didn't seem likely that Vintain would be mixed in with some sort of inmate population, but I couldn't be sure. I'm glad to hear he's had plenty of time alone to think about what an asshole he's been.

The door groans on its hinges as Loctulan swings it open. "Tonorf will assist you from here."

I remember the name, of course. Tonorf was one of Revlen's men who I met at the Gilded Gargoyle. It makes sense that one of her most trusted would be assigned to keep an eye on Vintain.

Loctulan locks the door behind us as we enter another chamber. It's bright as day in there, with so many torches lining the walls that my pupils dilate. As my eyes adjust, I see Tonorf, where he stands waiting for us to walk forward. Beside him, there's a wall of bars. Behind those bars, sits Vintain, who stares right at me as if he's been waiting for this moment all along.

CHAPTER 23

"It's okay," Tonorf says. "He won't bite."

"He would if he could," Revlen says. She walks forward and the rest of us follow, although it takes me a moment to set myself in motion.

"True," Tonorf says, as we draw closer, "but we took his teeth out." He turns to me, looking suddenly self-conscious. "Well, to be more precise, you did."

"It wouldn't have been possible without your bravery," I say.

I'm not being modest; it's just true. If Revlen and her men hadn't thought to keep me safe while Vintain hunted for me, chances are I wouldn't have been around when the time came to turn the tables. Still, my eyes keep flicking to where Vintain sits just a few feet away. He's no longer looking at me now, or even out at us as a group. He sits at a table in his brightly lit cell, staring down at something I can't see.

My eyes go from Vintain, to Tonorf, and then to Esras. "Wait, can he not...?"

"Look closer." A smile tugs on Esras's lips.

I check Vintain's cell again, now seeing what I didn't before as my eyes adjusted to the glare. Across the bars, there's a nearly invisible shimmering curtain.

Tonorf grins, as if fighting the urge to laugh. "Don't worry. You're not the first to miss it. The wards here are both extensive and complex. That one allows us to see in, but not him to see out. Same goes for sound, unless we choose otherwise."

"As you can see," Revlen says. "Everything's fine. The rat remains in his trap. Come on, let's get a better look."

We're just a few feet away already, which seems close enough for me. As it is, my skin crawls at the sight of him. Still, I'm the one who insisted we come here.

As a group, we step closer, the only thing between us and Vintain those bars and a nearly transparent field of magic. It's like we're visiting a human zoo, and I guess in a way we are—this exhibit dedicated to one of the realm's most dangerous predators.

The cell is simple, in many ways the same as those you'd see in a human prison. Although, it's slightly larger, with a bed, a chair and table, as well as a small barred window. I'm not really sure what those bars are for, since we're so high up in the air. To prevent suicide, possibly, although in this case it seems unlikely. To feel remorse or depression, you'd have to own a soul.

My eyes go to Vintain again, where he remains seated at the table. "What's he doing?"

Now that we're closer, I can see that he's holding cards shaped like hexagons. He keeps studying them, every so often setting one down before him, where he has others laid out in rows.

"It's called Lonsec," Esras says. "A card game played alone."

I glance over at him, and then back to Vintain. "Like Solitaire?"

He shakes his head. "I don't know what that is. If you say so, probably."

The scene before us is just so peaceful, and so strange, as Vintain sits playing his game. Still, my pulse remains elevated, and I tell myself it's a natural reaction to seeing my old enemy. All the same, it seems like my heartbeat should be starting to slow. Instead, my pulse keeps increasing, as an edginess keeps building within me. It just keeps getting worse, to the point where I'm startled when Esras next speaks.

"Well, there you have it," he says. "I don't know how to explain what you've been experiencing, but that snake can't have anything to do with it. His reign of terror is over."

The steel that creeps into Esras's voice makes me look at him. He keeps his jaw set hard as he looks at Vintain, his face tight with barely concealed hatred. After all, if it wasn't for Vintain and the world he created, Esras's family might still be intact. His little sister might still be alive.

I resist the urge to reach for his hand. "I know this can't be easy, coming here like this. I'm sorry."

Esras shakes his head at my apology. "There's nothing to be sorry about. It's perfectly understandable that you'd suspect him."

As always, he's kind, but I can't help wonder if he's thinking what I've suspected myself so many times. Namely, that what Vintain did to me left me too traumatized to think clearly. Still, I felt so sure. And what of that edginess that keeps getting stronger? Is that too just due to trauma?

I turn to Tonorf, gesturing toward Vintain. "Is he like this all the time? Does he just sit there playing cards?"

Tonorf shakes his head. "Not all the time, of course. At first, he was difficult to manage."

"I would imagine," Revlen says, her tone proud at having orchestrated Vintain's downfall. "He must have been furious."

Tonorf grins. "He was, believe me. He kept carrying on about controlling Faerie again. Saying he'd have all of us killed. Totally deluded, obviously."

Revlen nods, not surprised to hear it. "I'm sure it took a bit of time for his situation to sink in."

"A few weeks," Tonorf says. "Then he became more placid."

I keep staring at Vintain, where he sits oblivious to us watching him. He keeps staring at his cards, every so often slowly setting one down. "Is he on drugs?"

Maybe that's what's going on. I keep checking Vintain's eyes and it's like the wheels aren't even turning.

Again, Tonorf's shakes his head. "He hasn't had any medications lately."

For some reason, the back of my neck tingles in what feels like a psychic ping. It's definitely not one I'm going to ignore. "What do you mean, lately?"

Tonorf shrugs. "For a while he kept complaining of stomach pains. Keveris arranged for him to see the physician."

This seems to pique Revlen's curiosity too. "Who's the physician?"

I have to wonder if there might be a psychic side to her I don't yet know about.

"Nathic Cloethle," Tonorf says. "He was assigned here the same time as me."

I hate to ask, but I still do. "Is he Seelie or Unseelie?"

"Unseelie. Why?" Tonorf says.

I can feel Esras looking at me, but I can't meet his gaze.

"Just wondering if you knew him," I say, not forgetting my last faux pas. I really need to let go of that prejudice.

"If it was up to me, I would have let him suffer," Tonorf says. "But they let Nathic get him some medicine."

Not only don't I like the sound of that, but the back of my neck tingles again, this time strong enough that I have to keep myself from shuddering.

Apparently, Revlen gets another ping on her radar too, since she goes right where I was going. "And that was weeks ago, you said."

Tonorf nods. "Yes. After that, he settled down."

A few moments pass as Revlen considers, then she sighs. "Well, I guess he became resigned to his fate."

That idea doesn't sit right with me either. Honestly, I'm surprised Revlen is willing to ignore her instincts on this. Then again, she's not feeling the supernatural edginess I'm feeling on top of those psychic pings.

"As you can see, he's being watched carefully," Tonorf says. "Were there any more concerns?"

Revlen shifts her gaze to me, as does Esras.

I hesitate, reluctant, but I haven't got anything to go on. What can I say, that the back of my neck tingled? "I guess not," I say.

After a moment, Esras's eyes slide away from mine. "Then I guess we'll be going."

Revlen turns her attention back to her old friend. "Thank you, Tonorf."

"Of course. Just let me know if there's anything more I can do."

Tonorf starts walking across the chamber and we follow. We're almost at the door when something occurs to me. Until this moment, I've been ruling something out. I've just assumed it wasn't possible. All the same, there's no denying that the edginess I feel is a lot like what I felt the other day in Bethany's apartment. As well as at Byrd Park the other night, to a degree, but that was active energy and this feels more like lingering energy. More specifically, lingering *demon* energy. Where the hell is that coming from?

I step back from the others, taking a moment to close my eyes. Like I did the other night, I allow my perceptions to shift as I extend my supernatural feelers. I open my eyes to look at Vintain again, and this time I see it. There's an aura surrounding Vintain, pulsing and flickering with a fiery glow. The realization hits me like a punch to the stomach.

"He has magic," I say.

The others turn too, trying to see what I see. They can't, I know, so they're just going to have to take my word for it.

"That's not possible," Revlen says, "I assure you, the wards—"

"It's not fae magic," I say, my heart pounding at the sudden realization. "It's demon magic. That's how he's been doing it."

CHAPTER 24

A stunned silence follows my claim, as Esras, Cade and Revlen stare at me. I can see that they're not sure what to think. After all, they can't feel what I feel, or see what I see. At the same time, they're not strangers to magic, and they're definitely not strangers to the depths of Vintain's duplicity. They look to me to see what we should do next.

"We need to check him," I say. "He must have something."

Tonorf looks to Revlen for confirmation.

"She's right," Revlen says. "We need to check him. Can you lower the ward?"

Tonorf strides back toward Vintain's cell, where he raises both hands, his lips moving as he recites an incantation. The shimmering curtain fades as, finally, Vintain looks out past his bars. I brace myself for the moment of recognition, but it doesn't come. Vintain's eyes sweep over us, both curious and surprised, but there's no sign that he knows who we are. Which, in itself, is weird as hell.

"Stand up," Tonorf says, as he enters the cell. He grips the pommel of his sword, the blade partly unsheathed.

Without a word, Vintain rises from his seat. His gaze shifts from Tonorf, to us, and then back to his guard.

"Come out from behind the table," Tonorf orders. "Stand before me."

Calmly, almost robotically, Vintain does as he's been told. He steps out from behind the table and goes to face Tonorf. He's dressed simply in loose-fitting trousers and a plain shirt, what must be the fae version of a prison uniform. Neither appear to have pockets. I check his fingers for rings and his neck for a cord, but see no sign of anything that could hold magic.

"Tell him to take off his clothes," I say, although the last thing I want to see is Vintain naked.

Tonorf glances back at Revlen, his expression uncertain.

"Tell him," she says.

Tonorf turns back to Vintain. "Remove your clothes. Slowly. Shirt first."

Vintain's gaze shifts to us and then back to Tonorf. He still doesn't utter a word.

"Do it," Tonorf says. "You lost the right to be modest when you entered these walls."

Vintain nods, just barely moving his head. Slowly, he peels off his shirt to reveal a lean but well-muscled torso, his skin milky pale. I still see nothing he could use to counter the wards around him.

"Drop it to the floor," Tonorf says.

Vintain drops the shirt, which he's kept held bunched in one hand.

Tonorf steps closer. "Now turn around."

Again, Vintain nods and slowly starts to turn. Then, almost too quickly for my eyes to track, he spins and executes a series of motions of inhuman precision. Within an instant, he throws a blow knocking Tonorf off balance, grabs the pommel of Tonorf's sword, unsheathes it and drives the blade through Tonorf's gut. Tonorf no sooner drops when Vintain staggers back himself, his eyes wide with shock. He raises his hands to where the handle of a dagger now protrudes from his chest. As he too falls, I track his stunned gaze to see Revlen, whose arm still remains outstretched from the throw of her knife.

CHAPTER 25

Revlen rushes to where Tonorf lays on the floor and drops to her knees beside him. My gaze shifts to where, at the back of the cell, another man lays slumped against the wall. He wears no shirt, his hands still clutching the knife in his chest, his ribcage covered with blood. All the same, I can't look away. Whoever he is, I've never seen him before. While Vintain is pale, with nearly platinum hair, this man is bald with a dark complexion. So, that's what I was seeing before—that magical aura was some sort of glamour.

"Who the hell is that?" Cade says.

It's a damned good question.

Behind us, Revlen's voice rises in anger. "He's dead. The son of a bitch killed him."

There's no doubt that what she says is true. Tonorf lays still and pale, a pool of blood spreading around him. The question remaining is who, exactly, killed him? Unfortunately, that man also appears to be dead.

While my heart breaks for Tonorf, I can't contain an outburst of my own. "Goddammit! We need to know how this happened."

Revlen spins on her knees on the blood-soaked floor. "Get him onto the table. Now!"

At first, I think she has to mean Tonorf, but her gaze remains fixed on the stranger. For a moment, no one moves, but then Esras snaps out of his shock. He rushes across the room, Cade soon following after him. Together, they crouch near the stranger's body.

"Take hold of his legs," Esras says, wrapping his arm around the dead man's chest. He waits for Cade, and then says, "Now, lift him!"

I watch in horror as they carry the man across the cell, swinging his body to clear objects from the table. Then they drop him down onto his back.

Revlen rises from Tonorf's side, her hands and legs soaked with blood. She goes to where the other man lays and locks her hands onto his temples. She starts reciting an incantation. As a glowing light starts to swirl around her hands, I realize I've never seen her use magic. She couldn't before, as Vintain kept it out of reach for anyone but himself and the Seelie nobles.

I watch curiously, wondering what type of magic she's using. "Is she trying to bring him back?"

"Not exactly," Esras says. "It's called Daua, a form of Unseelie death magic. If performed quickly enough, it allows for communication."

At his words, my eyes widen. This sounds like veil witch territory, or a form of necromancy. "Do you mean with his spirit?"

Esras shakes his head. "Again, not exactly. If it works, Revlen will be able to access the words still held within him. Like echoes of who he was while still alive. However, the energy lingering within him will be fading fast."

At that same moment, Revlen speaks to the dead man. "Please tell us your name."

It seems impossible, but his mouth opens. He croaks out the words, "Nathic Cloethle."

"And you're the physician here," Revlen says. "Is that right?"

I notice that she doesn't use past tense, instead addressing Nathic like he's still alive. I can't help but wonder if she's trying to keep him from knowing the truth.

"Yes," Nathic's corpse says. "Why can't I move?"

"Because you're asleep," Revlen says. "This is a dream."

I was right; she's definitely trying to keep him calm.

Nathic's corpse nods, apparently accepting that explanation.

"Please tell me how you ended up in the prisoner's cell."

"Vintain placed a glamour upon me and trapped me here."

Revlen glances up at us as she tries to think against the ticking clock. She turns her attention back to the corpse. "Go back to when Vintain asked to see you. Please tell me everything that happened."

The corpse nods, its dead eyes fixed on the ceiling. It speaks in a flat monotone. "Vintain said he was sick. That was a lie. He wanted me to help him."

Revlen shakes her head, confused. "Help him do what?"

"He was creating a new city kingdom. He said if I helped him, I'd have great riches."

Revlen frowns, her hands still pressed to the dead man's temples. "And you believed him?"

"I wanted to believe him."

"Why?"

"I borrowed money from the Black Sky and I cannot pay them back."

Revlen closes her eyes, as if these words pain her. She softly says, "Oh."

Confused, I look to Cade for an explanation. "An illegal gang," he whispers. "Kind of like the mob in our realm."

Revlen resumes her questioning. "Did they threaten you?"

Nathic's corpse nods again. "They said they'd kill my family. Serving the wishes of the High Mage would make us safe again."

Damn, I can't help but feel bad for the guy. He must have been beyond desperate.

"I don't understand," Revlen says. "So, you agreed to the glamour?"

The corpse opens its mouth but no words come out. Revlen looks to us again, her worried expression saying that we're running out of time.

"Nathic," she says. "Please answer. Did you agree to the glamour?"

The corpse speaks more softly this time, his voice growing weak. "I agreed only to procure an object for him."

Come on dead man, keep talking. I'm sorry, but we really need you to do this.

Revlen raises her voice, trying to keep him from fading. "Please, Nathic! Stay with us. What was it and where did you get it?"

"A talisman. He had it at his country house."

There's something I didn't know, that Vintain had another house. I guess it makes sense, given how long he's been around. Still, the same trait that makes me love the Unseelie, only makes me angry now. They're too damned trusting. They should have burned that house down to the ground.

"What kind of talisman?" Revlen asks. "What power did it have?" When those questions don't get a response, she says, "Nathic, what did he use it for?"

Light surges at her bloodied hands as Revlen invokes more magic. Still, a few moments pass before Nathic next speaks, his voice growing even more faint.

"He used it to mark me. He used it to take on my form and trap me within his." The corpse finishes speaking in little more than a whisper, before letting out a soft drawn out groan.

Revlen keeps her hands locked onto the dead man's temples, as she tries one more time. "Nathic, stay with me! What do you mean by mark? What kind of mark?"

It's plain to see that it's a lost cause. Any energy that was left lingering in the man is gone.

Finally, Revlen lets go and steps back. "I'm not sure what he meant."

The thing is, I'm pretty sure I do, because an image just rose up in my mind. One from that night I've relived so many times now, as I've kept seeing those events from Nora's house playing over and over in my memory. I look at Nathic's exposed torso, checking his arms once more. I still see nothing, but it has to be there somewhere.

"Come on," I say. "We need to roll him over."

The four of us take hold of Nathic's body. As gently as possible, we roll him onto his stomach. Then we watch as, upon his back, the last fiery hues fade from a tattoo shaped like a serpent.

CHAPTER 26

For a few moments, no one speaks as we try to recover from our collective shock. Revlen, in particular, looks pale and shaken. Which makes sense, considering that she just saw a friend die, killed the magically possessed man who murdered him, and then used her own magic to reveal the last memories held within his corpse.

I try to process the meaning of what we've witnessed, along with the fact that I was actually right. Part of me hoped I couldn't be, that there had to be some other explanation. Unfortunately, that's not the case. Vintain is now out there somewhere, having gotten hold of magic to make his escape. On top of that, he used demon magic. How it came to be stored in a hidden talisman, I can't say, but in a way it's not all that surprising. As the High Mage of this realm, Vintain maintained a stranglehold on magic. And didn't Esras say he also controlled the magic of those allowed to visit? I have to wonder if, somehow, he siphoned some off for himself.

Suddenly, an icy chill ripples through me as something else occurs to me. Again, I hope to hell I'm wrong. "What about Abarrane?"

Esras's eyes lock onto mine, as behind me Revlen audibly gasps.

"She's on this same floor," Cade says. "Can we get to her?"

It seems a damned good question. Tonorf is dead and Loctulan locked the entrance to this wing when he left. Keveris, presumably, went back down to the ground. Are we trapped here?

I figure there's only one way to find out, so I summon my magic as I stride to the door. As always in Faerie, it kicks in strong, and I channel that magic into the same kind of force I'd use for deflection. Only, instead of creating a shield, I direct that energy outward to blow the door off its hinges. A cloud of dust billows up from the floor.

"I think we're good," I say.

With me in the lead, we run down the hall toward the opposite end of the tower, where one more door awaits. I take that one down too. I'm about to run through when Esras grabs hold of me, yanking me back.

He calls out into the room beyond. "Guard, it's Esras and Revlen. We have others with us. Please stand down!"

He pushes past me to enter first, Revlen following close on his heels. We follow then too, entering a chamber just like the one that held Vintain where a guard stands with his sword drawn. His eyes widen at seeing both interim leaders of Faerie before him.

Revlen takes another step forward. "Please lower your sword."

The guard does as she asks, but keeps it unsheathed at his side.

"What's your name?" Revlen asks.

209

"Stenak," he says. "What's happened?"

Revlen shakes her head impatiently. "You wouldn't believe me if I told you, but we'll just have to get back to that. Right now, we need to check on the prisoner."

He turns toward the cell. "But she's—"

"That's an order," Esras says, falling in beside Revlen. "The blocking ward, please lower it."

Like Vintain's cell, this one also displays a shimmering curtain of magic. Past the bars, a woman stands with her back to us where she gazes out the window. She's tall and thin, with long blonde hair flowing down the back of her dress. Beyond her, the sky continues to darken, holding just the red glow of sunset.

"I've lowered the shield," the guard says. "What should I do now?"

Understandably, he sounds both confused and wary. Fair enough. He may be in the presence of Faerie's interim leaders, but we just showed up unannounced to magically blow the door down.

"Open the cell door, and please keep watch," Esras says.

Stenak unlocks the cell and slides the door open. Then he steps away, taking the same position he held before.

The others look to me, their expressions both worried and curious. I shake my head to answer their unspoken question. I sense no magic in this room, either fae or demon.

As a group, we step forward, but even now it seems that Queen Abarrane doesn't hear us. No, not Queen

Abarrane, I remind myself. Prisoner Abarrane. A woman without station or power, dressed in a plain garment and stripped of all magic. But just how much she's changed only becomes evident when she turns around.

Esras told me that she must be very old, hundreds of years at least. Now, she nearly looks it. The fae don't age as we do, and I've yet to see one looking truly ancient. Until now. The woman who stands before us looks nothing like the frighteningly beautiful queen who tortured me. She has transformed into a crone, her face gaunt and wizened, her frame skeletal within her dress.

She looks us over, her blank expression barely shifting. "I'm sorry," she says. "I didn't hear you come in."

None of us speak, as a group presumably too shocked by her transformation.

The guard, Stenak, speaks softly. "She's pretty much gone now. Nothing she says makes sense."

Esras nods, his gaze fixed on the woman who was once Queen Abarrane. "Please tell us your name."

Abarrane looks at him briefly before her eyes go distant again. "Has the moon gone dancing again?" she says. "I keep waiting for the moon to start dancing."

Glances are volleyed back and forth between us, and then Esras tries again. "Tell us your name."

"The white hawk took roost with the lost children," Abarrane says. "They say his nest is forsaken."

Behind us, Stenak says, "She lost her mind when the regime fell. She's been that way since."

Actually, she was batshit crazy before, if you ask me. But could she be acting this way because she's not really Abarrane? That's what we were thinking before, but now I'm not so sure. My bet is that Vintain left the shell of his old queen right here to rot now that she's of no use to him. Not that she deserves any better, come to think of it. So, there may be one thing that Vintain and I finally agree on.

To be on the safe side, I try shifting my vision. Nothing happens. Not because my magic fails, but because there's simply no demon energy present.

"Some seeds only thrive in fire. Did you know that, dear?"

I realize that the question has been directed to me, and I look to see Abarrane's eyes fixed on mine. What's strange is that, while she no longer resembles the woman she was before, her eyes haven't changed. They remain the same two icy blue pools, a malevolent intelligence lurking in their depths. The only difference is that now she has no way to channel that evil out upon the world. No wonder she went bonkers.

I look away, only to hear Abarrane speak again. "Some seeds thrive only in fire, and the trees born of fire shall be the strongest."

Once again, her gaze remains locked on mine as, behind her, the window glows red. Creepy. Making it even more creepy is that, for a moment, I could swear that light outside looks just like—

"Obviously, we're wasting our time," Revlen says. "We should go."

No sooner does she say it than all hell breaks loose. Bells start clanging in alarm as the sound of men shouting rises from the prison yard. The red glow at the window flashes blindingly orange, followed by ear-splitting shrieks that cut through the air. Within seconds, the smell of smoke starts to permeate the chamber. We spin around at the sound of footsteps as Keveris careens through the door, his eyes wide in a face streaming with sweat. "The prison is under attack!"

On instinct, Esras grips the pommel of his sword. "What's going on? Who's attacking?"

"Demons! They've breached the *realm*!"

Behind us, demented laughter rises from Abaranne's lips to echo through the chamber. "See, didn't I tell you?" she says. "Some seeds thrive only in fire!"

CHAPTER 27

The Tower of Solitude might be the safest place to be during an attack. It's virtually impregnable from the ground and inaccessible from the air, unless you're being carried by a griffin. Ironically, Prisoner Abarrane should be just fine. On the other hand, we order the griffins to carry us down to the battle. This was actually my idea, quickly supported by Esras, Revlen and Cade. If someone has opened the gap—and clearly someone has—then I'll be needed to close it. Esras and Revlen are natural leaders, both battle hardened and fearless. Cade too insists on fighting, when Keveris wanted to fly us over the walls to safety. Whether we would have been safer is hard to say, but it doesn't matter. None of us would be seen leaving.

We descend through billowing smoke to the sound of men shouting and bells ringing. As soon as we land, we leap out of the carrier and start running, the griffins taking back to the sky. They don't get far.

My head snaps up as more screeching cries cut through the air. Like something from out of a nightmare, two winged demons swoop down from above. My eyes widen as I realize what it was we heard before in the tower. These are zarcaroths, only this time they're real. Within a moment, one impales a griffin with its razor sharp beak, shaking it loose to let it drop. The other zarcaroth swings its serrated tail to lop off the second griffin's head. The ground shakes as their bodies crash down behind us.

We reach the fighting, where at least thirty men have spilled out into the yard. They keep drawing back, their frenzied faces lit by a rising wall of fire. I see just two more demons, both tall and shaped like men with broad scalloped wings. That they're vastly outnumbered makes no difference since they're living, breathing flame throwers. They work in unison, pivoting back and forth as they spew out fire. Now I know for sure what set Bethany's building ablaze.

Esras and Revlen run into the mix with their weapons drawn. Keveris calls out to his men and one of them throws a sword, which is passed off to Cade. Now it's time for me to do my job. I set myself in motion to run along the outside of the melee, knowing what I'm looking for. It doesn't take long before I see it—a gap in the veil pulsing with a fiery glow. That's the good news. The bad news is that it's on the other side of the demons and beyond the protection of the men fighting them. Still, I need to get there. If I don't close that gap, the demons will just keep coming.

I start sprinting in that direction when another screech comes from the sky, followed by another. I look up to see the zarcaroths circling above me. Great. In all this mess, they just happened to lock in on me? I'm the smallest thing out here. I can't imagine it being a coincidence. Nonetheless, they're bearing down fast and, vampire workouts or not, I don't suspect I can outrun them. I spin around to stand my ground as Regina's words from training echo inside my mind. *One chance, one weapon!*

Well, in this case I need two chances, but I make my choice of weapons. Praying the ley line is with me, I ready myself as the first zarcaroth swoops in for the kill. My heart pounds and sweat drips down my back as I wait for it to draw closer. Then I snap out a crackling white-hot arc of energy to separate the zarcaroth's head from its body. Neither hit the ground. Instead, they burst apart in a shower of sparks as they leave this dimension. Apparently it's the same here as for demons on earth. What's not of this realm can leave no remains.

The other zarcaroth starts to fly up again, apparently thinking better of attack. My eyes become slits as I grit my teeth. *Forget about it, asshole. You're not going anywhere.* I strike out again, to take off a wing. Then I strike out once more to take off the other. I don't watch this time as the creature bursts apart. Instead, I say a quick and silent thank you to the ley line, and take off running.

I skirt around the outside of the fight, my eyes fixed on that gap in the veil. In a moment combining hope, training and pure desperation, I keep running full-bore and then launch myself into the air. For a moment, as I sail over the men, I feel sure I'm going to fall—but, somehow, both my levitation and trajectory stay true. I land on the other side of the flames and fighting, where I keep running and thrust out both hands. Twin shimmering orbs streak through the air, trailing white light in their wake. I brace myself, heart pounding and not sure what to expect. I'm in Faerie, after all. Can I even close the veil here? Then both orbs strike home, the veil gap imploding in a burst of blue light.

Gasping for air, I spin around and march toward my remaining two targets, who appear as huge silhouettes against the glow of the fire. They have their backs to me as they continue battling the men. They may think they're winning, but I just cut off their escape. I let out a scream of rage and thrust out twice more to release what might be the last of my magic. Hearing me, the fire demons spin in my direction, but it's already too late. My heart leaps in my chest as they become engulfed in a brilliant white light.

"Consider yourselves extinguished," I hiss, as they flail, stagger back and start to melt inward. A moment later, nothing remains but two smoldering husks that are already starting to fade.

Utterly depleted, I stumble back as my legs start to wobble. Then I hear voices rise from what feels like miles away. I turn in that direction and realize that what I'm hearing are the men shouting, cheering and calling my name. Beyond the now dying wall of flame, they hold up their swords, thrusting them up toward the sky. In the crowd, I see Revlen and Cade, both of them grinning. Then I see Esras, his gaze full of pride and amazement as he too holds up his sword in salute.

Suddenly, I feel unsteady again and I stumble back once more. Then the scene before me fades to be replaced by a vision. I see a woman bathed in soft, glowing light as she stands within a misty void. She's tall and graceful, her long blonde hair falling upon the shoulders of her flowing white robes. She has ears that taper to points, and luminous eyes that remain fixed upon mine. I know her, of course, this force who hasn't forgotten that I freed her.

"You must go," she says. "Your realm needs you."

I walk toward her to take hold of her outstretched hand. Then she draws me in, wrapping me in light as she transforms herself into a portal.

CHAPTER 28

A moment later, I emerge onto a city street where more demons appear to be having fun. A car burns at the side of the road as flames reach toward the trees lining the sidewalk. Several streetlights lay smashed and twisted, where they've been uprooted and cast aside like broken toys. I'm so sick of these overgrown toddlers from Hell.

A quick assessment determines that I'm facing three of the bastards. There's one of the ever popular fire-breathers, a bull demon type—and, well how about that—something new yet again. This one resembles a tank crossed with a porcupine. It's at least six feet long with tall spiky quills that crackle and flare with electricity. That's as much time as I have for observation before the demons spot me where I now stand panting and sweating. Naturally, they start heading my way, since I'm the only thing out here for them to gore, burn or eat alive.

Wait, the ley line sent me back here to face this alone? What the hell was she thinking?

No sooner do I think it than Beatrice blips in beside me. She's quickly followed by Regina, Harper, Blair and Alec. In a moment that would be comic—minus the demons—Beatrice and I look at each other and both say, "How did you get here?"

In her case, I suspect she means it literally. Although, I'm not sure how she knows I wasn't here a minute ago. On the other hand, I assume she and the others arrived via magic key. How they knew to come, I have no idea. Neither of us get an answer, since the bull demon chooses that moment to bellow out a roar. He drops onto all fours and gets ready to charge. Based on my experience, the street will soon be melting as he burns a path our way.

"Okay, team, this is what you've been training for! Now, do what needs to be done!"

With that, Regina flies up into the air. *Gosh, thanks, Regina.*

Then I realize that she just went after a zarcaroth circling above. *Um, sorry, Regina. I take it back.*

Beatrice doesn't leave us on our own either. Just the opposite, as she takes the lead and starts marching forward. She thrusts out her arms and crosses her hands over each other, palms spread outward. She begins a pushing motion while reciting an incantation. The progress of the demons stops immediately, as if they've just come up against an invisible wall. Which they have, apparently, a wall conjured by magic.

Alec goes next. He raises his hands and begins gesturing in a summoning manner like the one he used at practice to call in birds. Only this time, the sky starts to rumble eerily before unleashing a sudden torrent of driving hail. Within seconds, it starts hammering at the demons in a rapid-fire barrage so dense and furious that I can barely see through it. Impressive magic, to say the least. Once again, I can't help but wonder if Alec inherited his power from Sarah Wellingsford. Damn, my hatred of her runs so deep that even now she haunts my thoughts.

Hatred of his relatives aside, there's no doubt that Alec's magic is effective too. The hail works to drive the demons further back. The bull demon lets out another roar, this time one of anger and confusion. I take that as a cue to get my ass in gear. I start running around the outside of both Beatrice's shield and Alec's machine gun wall of hail. Seeing that I'm already spent, I'm going to have to get close. The way I figure it, I need to take out three demons nearly simultaneously. It's going to take a lot of supernatural juice, and I'm not even sure if I have any left.

I'm almost at an opening when I nearly collide into a row of figures wearing long, hooded robes. There's at least ten of them coming at the demons from the side, all of them firing lightning bolts from their hands. They have to be wizard-class mages, but where the hell did they come from? I circle back behind Alec and Beatrice, thinking I'll come at the demons from that angle. The same thing happens again, as another row of hooded figures suddenly appears. I hit the brakes and shake my head, baffled. Then my eyes widen as the hooded figures start growing taller. Within seconds, the demons are penned in by two looming walls of giants. This must be a demon's nightmare.

Suddenly, something occurs to me. Holy shit. Is that even possible?

My eyes cut to Blair who, sure enough, stands with her knees bent, her hands spread wide and her eyes rolled back into her head. Now I know what I'm seeing. Those mages aren't real—they're magical manifestations provided by Blair, as she taps into the demons' collective fears. Apparently, she's taking anxiety issues to a new level.

While I've never seen demons show fear, now they seem panicked. The porcupine tank keeps spinning in circles, it's spiny hackles raised and shooting off electrical charges. It can't tell who's real and who's not, so it can't tell who to fire upon. The bull demon rises onto its massive hind legs, raising clenched fists to the assaulting sky. His eyeballs are literally on fire as he impotently rages. Meanwhile, the fire-breather stands hunched and spewing a steady stream of flame as hail keeps pelting against him. Unlike his rodent pal, he's chosen a target.

That target is Harper, who stands with her legs braced and her hands thrust out before her. For a moment, I think she's preparing to unleash a firestorm of her own, but that's not what's happening. She's collecting the demon's fire into herself to keep the rest of us protected. Her entire body is engulfed in a blazing glow, her skin scarlet. Her normally hazel eyes have become two obsidian pools of furious concentration.

It's a surreal moment in which I realize what's happening. Those around me are working in concert to keep the demons distracted, deceived and, amazingly, afraid. They've created the opening. Now I need to do my job and usher the Hell toddlers back out of here again.

The realization galvanizes me with a fresh, and seemingly impossible, rush of new magic. It's not Faerie ley line supercharged, but I think I can do this. I dash straight through the wall of illusory wizard giants just as the hail finally quits. My guess is that Alec dialed that back so I wouldn't get battered.

I have three demons to choose from, so I choose the electric rodent first. The way I figure it, all it will take is one of those quills to skewer me. Sensing my approach, it spins around, hackles raised and taking aim. I launch an orb in the same moment that the rodent fires off a charge. His shot goes wide while mine hits the bullseye. The oversized prickly critter squeals, starts shuddering like crazy and goes into a crackling electrical seizure. I run past, ducking and covering, as the thing explodes and sizzling quills shoot through the air.

One down and two to go.

This time, I choose the fire-breather. I'm just not sure how much longer Harper can hold that fucker off. Thankfully, he doesn't see me coming up behind him as I close in for the strike. I unleash orb number two. Yes! This time the demon gets sucked back toward me, as if by a vacuum, the orb expanding around him. A moment later and he's demon dust, the last stream of fire to leave his mouth still streaking through the air.

Just one to go now and we can call it a day. Thankfully, I seem to be on a roll. No sooner do I have that thought than I'm picked up into the air and slammed to the ground. The breath leaves my lungs with a sudden whoosh. For a moment, I'm too stunned to move. Then I spin onto my back just as the bull demon drops down from his hind legs to pin me.

Shit. That's what I get for acting cocky.

The bull demon clenches my wrists in his two massive hands, driving my arms into the asphalt. I scream out in pain, thrashing my head back and forth as I wriggle my legs. I can wriggle them all I want. I'm not going anywhere. The demon looks down at me with fiery eyes, his corkscrew horns gleaming in the moonlight. I stare pinned, helpless and terrified as a grin splits his face. Clearly enjoying the moment, he slowly rears back his head. In a sickening moment, I realize just what he has planned. He's about to drive those two horns right through me. In what I'm sure will be my final moment, I think of Autumn, then I close my eyes and prepare for the end.

Suddenly, the pressure against me is gone. My eyes pop open to see the bull demon reeling away backwards, as if caught by some sort of snare. Then I realize that's exactly what's happening. Wrapped around his throat is a winding noose of thick vine. That vine is connected to a long branch reaching all the way out from the sidewalk. That branch is connected to one of the trees lining the street. Beneath that tree stands Alec, his hands clenched into glowing fists as he reels that branch in, tugging the now choking demon like a fish on a line.

I leap to my feet, stagger forward and then start to run. With everything in me, I reach inside to summon more magic. As they say, failure isn't an option. It's only a matter of moments until the demon tears that vine from his throat. When that happens, Alec will die.

I light up another orb, and this time it's me charging the bull. I fix my fury on that bastard, let out a primal scream, and hurl my orb through the air. I deliver it with some serious gusto. I mean, come on, that asshole was on top of me. The bull demon bellows out one last roar and then gets obliterated, as burning chunks of demon beef go sailing through the air.

Alec drops to his knees.

Just a few feet away, I do the same.

Both of us grin at each other.

"Just so you know…" He pauses, breathing, hard, and then gestures to where our fellow witches rush toward us. "You guys *are* my family these days."

I nod, panting and sweating, his comment hitting home. Here I've been, angry at the unfairness of others judging me and Autumn, while I've being doing the same thing to him. Only, instead of ancient witch lore, I've based my prejudice on something way more flimsy.

"I'm an asshole, aren't I?" I say.

Alec shrugs, that grin still on his face. "Sometimes, yeah. But you have some good qualities."

"I'll keep working on those."

Alec nods. "I figured you would. Are we good now?"

"Yeah," I say. "We're definitely good."

Then I jump as something slams down to the ground behind me. I turn to see an unconscious zarcaroth. Above it, Regina hovers in the sky.

"Hey, veil witch," she says. "Take care of that, will you?"

Apparently, this is both my night to win a few rounds and also get put in my place. I gather myself up, conjure one last orb, and go do as I've been told.

CHAPTER 29

As Autumn and I sit at her kitchen table watching YouTube, her jaw drops open and her eyes go wide. I was there, and I'm nearly having the same reaction. The footage is grainy, blurry and taken from a distance—probably by someone in one of the downtown buildings. Still, you can make out burning cars, driving hail, and the hulking forms of the demons. Arcs of fire streak across the street as bolts of electricity crackle up into the air. Just before the video cuts off, you can see the small scurrying forms of people running toward the threatening creatures.

Autumn looks up from the laptop. "Seriously, that was you?"

I nod, rubbing my sore arms once again. Fucking bull demon. "Well, us. Those were the Shadow Order guys I told you about. I would have been baked without them." More than likely, literally.

Autumn shakes her head briskly. "There were a bunch of stories about some gas main exploding."

I shrug and take a sip of my coffee. "Pretty sure that happened later."

The fact is, I know it happened later. As soon as we dispatched the demons—and with the sound of sirens bearing down quickly—Beatrice used one of her magic keys to open a portal. A spinning circle of sparks suddenly appeared beside her.

"Get through that now!" she said. "We'll be right behind you."

She meant herself and Regina, of course, although we weren't sure why they were staying. That portal spit us out miles away, up by Capitol Square. Why there, I have no idea. Beatrice had been acting fast, so maybe she just chose a local key at random. As the four of us started walking, we speculated on why Beatrice and Regina might have stayed behind. We decided they were probably going to find a way of covering things up. This morning, I saw the stories about the gas main explosion.

Autumn looks at me, her eyebrow cocked. "Did you read the comments?"

She points to where, beneath the now stilled video, the list of comments keep growing longer.

"Yeah, I saw those," I say. "Of course it's a hoax, right? I mean, come on. Demons?"

"Of course. No such thing." Autumn looks at the screen again, a smile playing on her lips. "I particularly like this one," she says, and then reads the comment. "You expect us to believe that some idiots actually ran at those monsters? Go back to film school, asshole."

She starts laughing and I do too.

"Right, I'm one of the idiots," I say.

"I like that part best," Autumn says. "Kind of true, actually."

Which only makes us laugh harder. That we can laugh at all only goes to show that we're in denial. Right now, we definitely shouldn't be laughing. Tomorrow night, Autumn will stand trial before the supernatural community. And the location for that particular event? Sarah Wellingsford's estate, of course. Meanwhile, Bethany and the others remain in limbo, and some asshole witch keeps opening the veil. Oh, and Vintain is on the loose again. Things are going great.

Done laughing, we fall silent for what I think will be a moment. Then the silence lingers, and I brace myself for where we have to go.

Finally, Autumn closes her laptop and looks at me. "So, how's Esras doing?"

I shake my head, confused. "That's what's on your mind?"

Autumn nods, as if there's no reason to be thinking of anything else. "Just curious. You didn't really go into that part. Was he, like, happy to see you, or more like all business?"

I blink at her a few times. "We went to a prison."

"So?" That smile starts tugging at the corner of her mouth again.

"Well, I mean, it wasn't like we went out for a romantic dinner."

"I know, but you can still tell."

I squint at her like she's insane. "We ended up battling demons."

"Yeah, I know. You told me. How was the vibe between you two?" Autumn takes a sip of her coffee.

"At the prison, while we fought demons," I say. "Just making sure I'm getting this right."

Autumn just nods, keeping her eyes on mine. Her expression says, *Take your time and think about it. I'm not in any rush.*

So, I think back to last night. Despite everything that happened, two moments come to mind above all others. The first is when we were getting out of the freaky griffin elevator and Esras made sure I was okay. Well, and also made me accidentally horny just by placing his hands upon my midsection. The second is his face lighting up in a triumphant grin when I took out those demons. Even now, just thinking about his fond admiration sets my heart to pounding. Weirdly, everything between those two moments feels hazy by comparison.

I bring my gaze back to Autumn's. "The vibe between us was good."

Her eyes grow warm. "So, like really good, or so-so good?"

I can't believe it, but I feel myself smiling again. I shrug and say, "Well, it's not like we started banging in front of everyone, but it was really good."

Autumn laughs. "Yeah, well, I figured it probably didn't go that way. Still, good to know. What about Phoenix?"

Seriously? Of all the stuff we have to talk about? "You were there. No banging happened on that front either."

Autumn shrugs this time. "I wasn't there the entire time. You guys took that *walk*." She uses finger quotes.

"Which was a *walk*," I say. "Literally. Not 'walk' as in a euphemism for screwing."

Autumn rolls her eyes, reminding me very much of our mother in this moment. She even sighs. "Banging and screwing aside, how's the vibe there?"

"What's with you and the vibes today?"

Autumn shrugs again. "Indulge me."

So, I think back to that walk I took with Phoenix and the things we talked about. Immediately, his words come back to me from that peaceful, sad moment, during which I both wanted to cry and hold onto him forever. *Love makes witchcraft seem simple.*

My eyes start to mist, and it takes me a moment. Then I say, "The vibe was good there too."

Autumn reaches for my hand across the table, placing hers upon mine. "Oh, geez," she says.

"What?" I say, but already a tear is running down my cheek. I use my free hand to wipe it away, hoping she didn't notice, or that maybe I can pass it off as cat allergies or something.

Autumn hesitates, but then says, "I thought it might be more cut and dried."

I shake my head. "Probably not."

"Oh, baby."

And just like that, my tears start falling, even as I'm so totally pissed off at myself. Am I really crying over this when my sister's life will be on the line tomorrow night? Apparently, yes.

"I'm sorry," I say. "I'm ridiculous."

Autumn scoots her chair closer and then wraps her arms around me. She strokes my hair while I cry. She speaks in a soft voice. "No, you're not ridiculous. You're tough as nails. Do you remember when we were kids, and we used to watch the Powerpuff girls?"

Now, I'm both crying and laughing as I remember those days from so long ago. Once upon a time, Autumn and I were just two little girls. Our parents were still young. Our father was still alive. The only monsters we knew of existed as animated characters on TV.

"I remember," I say.

"You said I was like Buttercup," Autumn says.

"Oh, my God, Buttercup. How do you remember?"

Autumn's eyes meet mine and she doesn't have to answer. She remembers because I was stolen. I went away and for fifteen years she searched to find me.

"You said I was like Buttercup because she was the tough one," Autumn says. "Because I was older than you."

I nod as Autumn holds onto me.

She kisses me on the forehead and says, "You're Buttercup. You're the kickass Powerpuff girl."

I start laughing again as I wipe my eyes. "You're totally Buttercup too."

"No," Autumn says. "I may be level-headed like Blossom, or maybe I'm more like Bubbles. She was the softie."

I think of how kind and patient Autumn has always been with the spirits she encounters, when I'm more likely to ignore them. Then again, of the two of us, she's definitely more level-headed and cautious. "You're kind of like both," I say.

Autumn nods. "That's okay. I can live with being a Bubbles-Blossom hybrid."

"Are you sure?" I say. "We could take turns. I can be Buttercup for a while, then you be Buttercup. I'm okay with that too."

Autumn pulls back from our embrace, keeping her eyes on mine. "You may just have to be Buttercup. That might just be the way it goes."

I start shaking my head as her meaning sinks in. "No."

"Cassie, you might just have to be. And, listen, you're way tougher than me. You know that."

I keep shaking my head. "No, no, no."

"Oh, sweetie." When I look up again, I see that Autumn's tears are falling now too, even as she smiles at me. "I looked everywhere to find you again. Then I found you. Do you think I have one worry about my life ending?"

"No, no, no."

"Because I don't. My life ended when you got taken. It began again when you came back. I'm fine. I'm more than fine. My husband died. I died too. Remember? But then I came back. You're *why* I came back."

"No, no," I say. "No."

Autumn wraps her arms around me again. She shushes me and says, "Everything will be fine. I know it will. But, listen, we need to talk about this now. We can't just pretend it's not there."

I try wiping my eyes, but it doesn't do any good. The tears just keep coming. I manage to say, "I know."

"This time I'm serious. Will you look after Louie?"

I look around for Autumn's one-eyed cat. I spot him sleeping in the corner, which is a little unusual. Typically, he comes around at night, and I have to wonder if he's staying close because he senses something. With all of my heart, I hope I'm wrong.

I shake my head. "Nope."

Autumn rolls her eyes. "And Mom. She's going to need you. Promise you'll be there for her."

Again, I shake my head. "No. I suck at that stuff. You're going to be there for her."

"Cassie, come on," Autumn says. "Stop screwing around. You're Buttercup, remember? You're the tough one."

Finally, I nod. "If something happens, I promise I'll be there for Mom and your freaky cat."

Across the room, Louie looks up and glares at me. Again, I think about witches having familiars. Could he possibly be...?

"Good," Autumn says. "Thank you. I knew you would be."

I wipe my cheeks again. "But that's not what's going to happen. My plan is to figure this mess out and be the first one to dance at your wedding."

Autumn raises her eyebrows. "Can you even dance?"

I shake my head, a grin tugging at my lips. "No. I didn't happen to have a body when everyone else was learning."

A strange moment of silence passes between us and then Autumn snorts. She tries not to laugh, but can't quite pull it off.

"It's not funny!" I say.

"Yeah, it kind of is," Autumn says. "I'm sorry."

Then I start laughing too. Because in a super weird way, it is funny. "Talk about body issues," I say.

Autumn starts laughing harder. "Well, at least you weren't obsessed about your weight."

I huff. "Right, because I didn't have any."

Autumn keeps laughing.

"Guess what I wore to the prom," I say.

Autumn's shoulders convulse as she shakes her head. "Julia!"

"Oh, my God," Autumn says. "You're killing me."

I level her with a stare. "Seriously?"

"Okay, that might not be the best choice of phrasing."

"That's okay," I say, as we both finally stop laughing. "Because no one is going to kill you. You're right, I'm Buttercup. And Buttercup always comes through in the end. That's what she does, right?"

Autumn looks at me with sad eyes. "Yes, that's what she does."

I get up from the table and grab my keys. "So, I guess that means I better get moving."

"Okay," Autumn says. "I guess you better."

But Autumn's sad gaze says that she knows I'm just grasping at straws. If I haven't figured this mess out over the last few days, two more isn't likely to make much difference. She walks me to her door and we look at each other one more time. Then Autumn wraps me in a tight hug, squeezing hard and holding me close like she may never be able to hug me again. And the fact is, she could be right.

"Go on, Buttercup," she says. "Get on out there and kick some ass."

I manage to make it all the way back to my car before I start crying again.

CHAPTER 30

Despite my tough act in front of Autumn, internally I'm freaking out. The clock is ticking so loud I can barely think. Meanwhile, I'm running out of options. As I've done so many times in the last few days, I go over the things I know, once again hoping to see the connections that somehow keep eluding me.

I know that Silas killed Nora's friends, apparently at Mason's bidding. But was that just to frame one of us? To carry out a vendetta on Mason's behalf? Both?

I know that Mason is in league with the demons, but I'm not sure where Silas fits in there. Or, for that matter, if he even does.

I know that Nora's friends being killed allowed Sarah Wellingsford to pin the crime on Autumn. Although, my gut still says she'd rather it was me. I just happened to have an alibi. At the same time, I don't know how Sarah's grudge ties into Silas's grudge against us. Or, once again, if it even does.

I know that Vintain has escaped, from the sounds of things weeks ago. I know that he knew about Silas. I'm also pretty damned sure it was Vintain's magic I went up against in that portal house of mirrors. Again, though, I don't know how Vintain is connected to Silas now, or what his plan could possibly be. What could Vintain, demons and a group of vampires all have in common? Other than the fact that they're nuts, of course.

Finally, there's a high demon named Nepheras, who seemed just fine with Mason and his vampire followers being in her realm. Which tells me she must also know about Silas, and quite possibly Vintain. Or maybe I'm entirely wrong.

At the end of it all, I'm left with one big snarled up ball that never quite seems to unravel. I keep pulling at it, kicking at it and throwing it around, but what's at its center remains hidden.

Letting out a cry of frustration, I slam my hand against the steering wheel. My car veers and I pull back just in time to avoid hitting a tree. "Easy, Cassie," I say to myself. "You won't do Autumn any good if you're dead."

Not that I seem to be doing her much good now. I may be many things, but apparently I'm not a detective. Ironically, I know a detective, but I can't ask him for help. I swore to Autumn I wouldn't tell Ian, although once again I wonder when she's going to tell him herself. Is it that she just can't bring herself to do it?

Or, to protect him, is she simply never going to tell him and just disappear from his life? That's something I can see Autumn doing. Yes, part of him would die. Part of him would forever hate her for having lied to him. At the same time, she'd meet her end knowing she never put him up against something he had no way to handle. In fact, something that could get him killed. This way, he'd survive, and that might just be the best Autumn can do right now.

I get to where I'm going and pull over to the side of the road. I take a deep breath to keep myself from crying again and I reach for my phone. I pause for a minute, ready to send a text, but not quite sure what to say. I glance out at the darkness that just settled in beyond my windshield, and decide to go with the absurd.

Are you up yet?

A minute passes, my phone buzzes, and I read Nora's response. *Just woke up. How'd you guess?* That along with a fanged emoji smiley face. There are customized vampire emojis? It's kind of cool, actually.

I fire off another text. *I was thinking I might head out with you guys tonight.*

Nora will know what this means. Namely, that I keep coming up dry and remain desperate for clues. Which I'm sure she suspected, since I would have told her otherwise.

Nora texts back a second later. *Okay. I'll be down in a minute.*

I imagine sensing a weary disappointment in her words, reminding me that all of this has been hard on her too. After all, my sister remains alive and there's still hope I can save her. Nora can't say the same for those she lost. All she can hope for is some form of justice. So, in a sense, she's relying on me too.

Soon, we're heading upstairs to where, these days, she's squatting along with her vagabond vampire buddies. It's almost unexpected now, but my skin still starts to prickle. It's strange to think that, even though I know these people, these instincts still kick in. Is there any way to stop that from happening? Honestly, I don't think so. It's just the way I'm wired. Like it or not, it's something I have to live with.

The scene inside their shared dwelling is exactly the same as last time. John and Eric sit playing video games, while Stephanie stares at her phone. They appear both relaxed and bored, and it strikes me just how normal their actions seem. Pretty much what you'd expect from any group of people in their twenties. Of course, in this case at least one of them is well over a hundred. Still, it makes me wonder what I used to imagine vampires doing in their off time. Filing their fangs? Hanging from the rafters like bats? I never gave it much thought, just always thinking of them as human-shaped ticks who lived forever if I didn't step on them.

"Hi guys," I say, following Nora into the room.

"Hi Cassie," Stephanie says, like she's known me for years.

"Hey, we saw your show," John says, clicking away madly on his controller.

I'm not quite sure if he's talking to me until Stephanie makes eye contact. "He meant the YouTube thing. That was you, right?"

Out there in the world are all those who left nasty comments beneath the video, calling the person who uploaded it a hoaxer. Meanwhile, I chat with a group of vampires who never doubted its authenticity.

"I was there," I say.

"Were those your Shadow Order peeps?" The question comes from Eric, who looks my way for a moment. He looks back at the screen and says, "Fuck!"

"Snooze you lose," John quips in a happy tone.

Vampires may be hard to kill in real life, but they die just like the rest of us in video games. At least that's what I guess must have happened, because Eric hangs his head and sighs. Then he looks my way again, signaling that he's still curious.

"Most of them," I say. "One wasn't caught in the video." I don't mention that she's a flying dwarf who was doing battle with an airborne demon reptile. Presumably, some things have to be seen to be believed, even if you're a vampire.

"Cool," Stephanie says. "I wish that guy had kept filming. I was hoping to see you in action."

I shrug, my cheeks warming a bit. "It wasn't any big deal. We just sort of showed them the door."

"Still," Stephanie says.

"Same here," John says. "Hey, you should take some video of your own. You could have a kickass YouTube channel."

"Cassie the Demon Hunter," Eric intones in an attempt at baritone.

"I'd totally subscribe," John says.

"Me too," Stephanie says, her eyes not leaving me as she adds, "I'm hungry."

Wait, did she just go from imagining me having a YouTube channel to imagining having me for dinner? I feel myself blush even more, which apparently Stephanie notices. She laughs and says, "Sorry. I probably shouldn't have strung those two thoughts together. You coming with us for another ride-along?"

"I was thinking I might," I say.

Stephanie shrugs like it's fine with her. John and Eric seem unfazed too, as the sound of their video game mission continues in the background.

The fact is, I wasn't sure how the idea would go over, but I guess they got past that demon attack. They must have realized it wasn't my fault. On top of that, they probably don't love the idea of a vampire-killing veil witch being on the loose. Especially one working with inside intel on where to find victims. As Nora mentioned, these vagabond types are low in the vampire pecking order. Who's to say if Mason might suggest them next for target practice?

So, come to think of it, there might be a few more people counting on me to settle the score. If only I knew how to make that happen, I guess we'd all sleep easier. The main difference being that some of us sleep at night, and some of us sleep during the day. The weird thing for me is that, right now, that seems like possibly the biggest difference between us. Well, that and subsisting on human blood, but even that doesn't seem like that big of a deal.

When all of this is over, I'm definitely getting therapy.

~ ~ ~

Before long, we're riding a bus across town again. I came close to offering to drive us, but then something occurred to me. I really don't need blood all over the seats if someone forgets to wipe their hands. The definition of dinner with friends has definitely changed.

The bus is quiet tonight, with the five of us grouped in a pod, me sitting beside Nora again. Up ahead there's a smattering of people, both couples and people alone, a woman reading a book with her young daughter—all of them oblivious to the fact that a group of vampires sits just a few feet away.

I can't help but wonder what it must be like for those I'm with. At some point, they were human too. They had their share of all that meant—joy, sadness, love and heartbreak, family and friends, hopes and dreams, visions for some sort of future. I don't want to think it, but I still do. I just can't help it. Will Autumn find herself in that same place soon? What will that mean to us? Will my hackles instinctively raise in the presence of my own sister? Will I have to fight against the urge to remove her from the realm?

I feel my eyes growing misty, which I can't have right now. I reach down, checking the sheath at my ankle, but taking a moment to lift the athame up just long enough to touch my fingertip to the blade. I feel it bite against my skin, that brief flash of pain reminding me that I'm human. My heart beating and pumping blood. For now, and there's no telling how long that might last, but that's the time I have. I need to find a way to protect my sister's time too.

"What's on your mind?"

I glance over at Nora. Such a simple question, which at the same time seems so intimate. She's never asked me before.

So, I answer honestly. "My sister."

"You must be worried," Nora says, her voice soft.

I nod. I let a few seconds pass. "And the things I've done." Which I wasn't aware of consciously, but it's always there when I'm around Nora.

"You mean to people like me," she says.

People like me. But, of course, she still thinks of herself that way. Why wouldn't she? Wouldn't I? Wouldn't Autumn?

I nod again. "Yes."

I almost jump when Nora places her hand on mine. It's not exactly cold, but it's not warm either. Then our eyes meet and it doesn't matter.

"Can I ask you something?" Nora says.

I hesitate just briefly. "Of course."

"At those times, did you feel that you did something wrong?"

I think for a moment, then shake my head. "No, but—"

"Don't do that to yourself." Nora keeps her eyes on mine. "Listen, I may not look like it, but I've been around for a long time. I know a bad person when I see one."

It's not the reaction I expected, but I find myself fighting off tears again.

I'm embarrassed when Nora notices, but she just says, "That's why, right there. You care. You feel. You have a big heart. I may not know you, but I know you. Okay?"

When I don't say anything, she says it again. "Okay?"

I nod. "Yes."

"And let me tell you this, young lady."

That one catches my attention. Is she reminding me that she's a century old teenager? The smile curling her lips tells me that's exactly what she's doing.

"Yes, ma'am?"

"Good, you're listening. And it's a simple message. There are two kinds of people, good and bad. The same goes for vampires. No different." She taps her chest. "Human at heart, all of us. So, those vampires you keep thinking about when you're around me? Stop thinking about them. Because if that was truly who you are, you wouldn't be sitting here."

In the end, I lose the battle against the tear. It runs down my cheek, but just the one before a smile tugs at my mouth too. "Did you just school me?"

"You bet I did." Nora looks out the window and says, "Let's try this. Do you mind pulling the cord? I'm starving."

I wrap my jacket around me as we get off the bus. There's a brittle chill to the air tonight, and a ring around the moon making me think of snow. We cross the street and enter another one of the city parks, John, Eric and Stephanie walking ahead of us. I suddenly realize this is the same park where I got off the bus that night thinking I'd seen veil witch magic. I know now that I was right. It's also where I faced off against that demon with at least one too many things protruding from his body. I shudder just thinking of his wide jaw dripping with goop, his glowing eyes and his all to obvious excitement at seeing me.

"The pickings here can be a little slim," Nora says, "Usually, just a few winos. That sort of thing. Still, it's worth a try."

I glance once more at our surroundings, then look over at her again. I lift an eyebrow.

Nora frowns, seeing my expression. "What?"

"No one says winos anymore."

"Like I said, I've been around for a while. But, fine. Maybe we'll run into a few drunks. Better?"

"Not exactly what I was going for."

Nora laughs, which isn't something I've heard often. But then, she's had a sad life. Or she *had* a sad life, depending on how you look at it.

"Anyway, we'll just have a quick look. After that, we'll hit a few bars."

By which she means scout for food, of course. Evidently, humans drinking alcohol plays a major role in how vampires score their meals. Which makes sense, when you think about it. That's when we're more likely to let our guard down, to take chances, to maybe cut through an alley or walk alone through a park. And, of course, while vampires possess a certain level of mind control, it works even better against an already compromised mind.

"I've been meaning to ask about vampires hanging out in bars or clubs. How does that work?"

Nora shakes her head. "What do you mean?"

"How do you manage to fit in if you never eat or drink anything?"

"We can drink," Nora says. "That's a total myth." She points to her mouth and adds, "See this hole right here? I just pour the wine right in there like everybody else."

I have to laugh at her choice of phrasing. "Do you feel it?"

"Not most of the time. You can't have a blood alcohol count without blood. But if we just so happen to feed off of someone who's got a good buzz going, that's a different story."

Okay, so maybe there's another reason why vampires prey on those who've been drinking. Who knows? Maybe that's the main reason. But, wait. Obviously, vampires drink blood. Now, I know they can also drink other things. Does that mean vampires pee?

I decide not to ask, instead opting for, "What about food?"

Nora shudders. "Technically, yes, but it comes right back up again. Definitely not worth it. For a while, most vampires still crave food, but that's entirely psychological. A month or so into the game, and just thinking about it makes you want to upchuck."

"Upchuck?"

Nora laughs again. "Okay, vomit, hurl, whatever. I keep slipping tonight, which means maybe I'm getting a little too relaxed."

She doesn't say it, but I know she means when she's around me. I guess that same aspect is true for me too, in that I can be around her without feeling too edgy. The feeling never goes away entirely, but I can at least push it to the background.

"I don't think anyone is out here tonight," Stephanie says, looking back at us.

Nora shrugs. "All right. Let's hang a right up here and loop back again."

Stephanie sighs. "Wish I was a rich vampire so I could keep a few blood bags in the fridge."

"We don't have a fridge," John says.

"Wish I was a rich vampire so I could have a fridge," Stephanie says.

John laughs.

Eric, on the other hand, seems distracted. He keeps looking around as if scanning for something. We walk for another minute, following a bend in the path, and then the others start doing it too.

I turn to Nora again. "What's up?"

She holds up a hand, signaling for me to stay quiet. We walk a few more steps before my edginess, suppressed before, starts to escalate. It's not the prickly demon energy I'm picking up on, that sensation which makes my skin crawl. Instead, I'm pretty sure it's more vampires.

Stephanie turns to look at the others. "That's Michelle, right?"

"I thought that was her," Eric says. "It sounds like she's influencing someone."

"Doesn't sound like it's working," Nora says.

I keep straining to hear, but we have to walk a few more yards first. Then I hear it too, a woman's voice speaking softly in firm, measured tones.

"I *said* you will turn around and walk away from us," she says. "Now, do it."

"Sounds like she's in trouble," Stephanie whispers.

Then I hear another voice, a man's this time. "Guess what? That shit doesn't work on me."

Nora starts to slow, signaling for the others to do the same.

Stephanie shakes her head. "We need to help her."

Ignoring Nora, she picks up her pace. Nora sighs and does the same. A moment later, we come around the corner and stop.

Three people stand just off the path in a clearing between trees. Two of them appear to be a couple, or at least together. She's petite and blonde, the girl who must be Michelle, beside her a guy with brown hair. But it's the guy standing across from them who rivets my attention, my breath catching in my throat. He's young, lean and tall, his posture aggressive toward the couple he faces. But it's mostly his hair that I notice. Even at night, it shines silvery gray. It's Silas. It has to be.

"We didn't mean anything," the girl says. "We were just checking on you."

Silas steps closer to the couple. Light swirls around his hands, which for now he holds down at his side. "By 'checking on you,' I guess you mean sneaking up behind me."

The other vampire shakes his head. His eyes are wide, leaving little doubt that he sees the magic being summoned for the strike. "Seriously, we didn't mean to scare you."

"Really," the girl says. "We weren't going to hurt you."

I can guess what just took place. The vampires thought they'd found prey, this person out walking alone. And what Michelle said is probably true. At least in her mind, she really hadn't planned to hurt him. All the same, her attempts at reassuring Silas fail. He takes another step closer, the light of his magic pulsing stronger.

"Just so you know, you didn't scare me," he says. "I've got news for you too. You can't hurt me either. On the other hand…"

He lets his words trail off, and for a moment the silence lingers. Then, like a snake ready to strike, he takes one quick step back. He thrusts out his arm once and then twice, launching two pulsing orbs in quick succession. The vampires see what's coming, but it's too late to move. Light engulfs them and they cry out as they drop to their knees. They crumple inward, instantly starting to decompose.

Beside me, Stephanie cries out, her anguish echoing through the night. "*What did you do? Why would you do that?*"

Silas spins at the sound of her voice, his expression shocked at suddenly seeing us. I watch as that shock shifts to a look of malicious interest as, for a moment, he thinks we're all vampires. Then comes stunned recognition when his eyes finally find me. Another orb flares to life in his hand as I too summon my magic.

I turn to those beside me and yell, "Run!"

The vampires scatter as Silas launches his orb. I do the same, the two magical charges meeting between us in a fiery explosion. The released force blows me back to stumble and then trip to the ground. I scramble up again to see that Silas is not only still standing but advancing toward me. He keeps his eyes locked on mine, his face twisted with hate. "They said I wouldn't be strong enough yet, but maybe they're wrong."

I stride toward him. "Who told you that? Why?"

That's as far as I get before I'm lifted into the air, my throat tightening as I start to choke. Silas holds his hands out, clenched as if strangling me, his brow furrowed in concentration. From the back of my dazed mind, I register what's going on. The fucker is using combat magic, a type I haven't learned and wouldn't want to. Although, I have no doubt where he did.

"Who told me doesn't much matter," he says. "But why. Let's talk about that." Silas sneers at me, still holding me up in the air. "Maybe because you killed my mother?"

Shock surges through me as I struggle against his hold. I shake my head, trying to speak as I gasp for air.

"What's up?" Silas says. "You look a little surprised. Oh, I know. You thought because no one knew she was a veil witch, that no one would make the connection."

Again, I shake my head, my mind reeling. Part of me knows I need to fight back, while part of me remains too stunned to move.

"In fact," Silas says, "You thought that you and your sister would remain the only ones of your kind. That was the plan, right? To rule over the witches?"

I snap out of my stupor at the mention of Autumn's name. What this asshole thinks, or why he thinks it, isn't my problem. But I'm not going to leave him out there hunting my sister. With resolve comes focus, connecting me again with my powers. I thrust out my arms to launch a shockwave of energy. Silas hurtles backward and I drop to my feet. Then I start marching forward.

"Listen, shithead, you got that backwards. In this case, the *who* matters very much." I start punctuating my words with quick jabs of lightning, focused at Silas's feet to keep driving him back. "I'll just take a stab at it. One of them is an asshole named Vintain, the other some bitch named Nepheras. Am I getting warmer? Maybe even hot?"

Silas manages to steady himself, raising a glowing outstretched hand, but this time I'm ready. Before he can strike again, I shift magical weapons once more, this time choosing my energy whip. I crack it against the air above him, once, twice and then again. He winces and falls back.

"Listen, and listen good," I say. "I didn't kill your mother." Silas throws out his arms, forming an energy shield to block my attacks. Damn, he really is strong, his magic already rivaling my own. God knows where we'll be if that strength keeps growing.

I crack my whip again, making sure I have his attention. "Did you even read her Book of Shadows?"

A look of bewilderment crosses his face. His eyes dart nervously to mine, then away and then back again. "There's nothing there. The pages are blank."

For a moment I'm puzzled too, but then I make the connection. Lauren Flannery charmed her book so that only a veil witch could read it. Silas isn't just a veil witch. He's something more, his magic enhanced through some other source.

"First rule of magic," I say. "Just because you can't see something doesn't mean it's not there. I read your mother's book. Do you want to know how? By not being a total asshole!"

I crack my whip again to drive my point home, throwing all of my energy against his shield. The thing bursts apart in a shower of sparks. I lash out once more, using precision to land a light blow. Silas lets out a howl and grabs hold of his arm.

"Let's see if we can finish this with one more lesson," I say. "Your mother wasn't killed by a veil witch. She was killed by a changeling named—"

Suddenly, there's a roar against my ears as I'm struck by a blast of hot wind. This time I'm not just thrown, I'm catapulted through the air. My back slams into a tree and I fall to the ground, the air rushing out of my lungs. I lay there groaning for a moment, my ears ringing. Where the hell did that come from? I thought I had Silas beat, or at least licking his wounds.

I clamber to my feet to stagger back in Silas's direction, commanding the sheath to unstrap at my calf. I don't want to do it, but if I have to I'll drag his dead body to the trial.

"I don't know what it's going to take to make you listen," I say. "For the last time, I'm not the one who—"

I stop as his gaze locks onto mine. Silas's eyes, pale blue before, have shifted to an all too familiar jade green. The serpent tattoo on his arm, which I'd all but forgotten, now glows with fiery light. And the grin that splits his face, I've seen on another before—a face that's bone-white, scarred and framed by slender pointed ears. Behind him, a portal that wasn't there moments ago, now pulses with orange light. As Vintain looks at me through Silas's eyes, he raises a hand to his forehead to give me a quick, joking salute. Then he steps back into his tunnel, which starts closing around him, as he takes his veil witch with him.

CHAPTER 31

It doesn't exactly help that the setting for Autumn's trial is almost identical to that of my first and only coven meeting. We sit gathered in Sarah Wellingsford's atrium, the inky night sky beyond the glass above, and beneath it at least two-hundred floating flames. Unlike last time, those flames burn in a spectrum of different colors. Some glow white like candles, others in hues of green, blue, and purple. Instinctively, I know they're wards.

As I scan the gathered crowd, it's easy to see why those wards are needed. While last time this room held only witches, that's not the case tonight. Among us are vampires and werewolves, as well as some of the Vamanec P'yrin, including Autumn's friends, Paul and Claudia. It's the custom, I've been told, in cases like this. In the event of a supernatural crime, the supernatural community has the right to witness judgement.

Suddenly, the flames surge, their light splashing across the glass above us. Then they lower, as their light again becomes muted. Beside me, Phoenix speaks softly. "That's the signal," he says. "It will start now."

At the far end of the atrium, the doors swing open at the hands of unseen witches. A hush falls over the crowd as my sister enters the room. She walks alone toward the dais erected for this occasion. She holds her head high, not looking around, even as I try to catch her eye to offer reassurance.

Next come the jurors, a group of ten witches supposedly chosen at random. Whether this is true, I can't say. All I know is that they don't look familiar. Then again, to be fair, I haven't spent much time around the larger witch community.

Next enters Isabel, who will be acting in Autumn's defense. She wears a flowing dress of pale green, which sets off her long golden hair. She too walks proudly, her gaze fixed straight ahead, looking very much like a queen of the witches.

Then a man enters the room. He's tall, with black hair graying just slightly at the temples. He's dressed formally, wearing an expensive dark suit. He is not a man I've seen before. Nor is he, strictly speaking, truly a man. His name is Phillip, and he's known to his kind as this region's arch vampire.

Finally, one more enters the atrium, the doors closing behind her. This is the witch of influence, the one who will both preside and, ultimately, pronounce judgement. Her name, of course, is Sarah Wellingsford.

As she passes before us, Phoenix gently places his hand on mine. It's a gesture of comfort, but also a reminder. He's right, of course, in that I seethe at the sight of the woman before me. It's all I can do to control myself, and those wards keeping our magic at bay are probably a good thing.

"Don't forget there's a jury," Phoenix whispers.

Again, the reminder is a good one, meant to set me at ease. The message being that the jury will make the determination, while Sarah's role is to decide on the sentencing. We already know the options there, all of them bleak. Still, this is a supernatural trial, which means I have no way of knowing what to expect.

The room remains silent as Autumn steps up onto the dais, taking the lone defendant's chair. She won't share a table with Isabel, who goes to stand behind one of three lecterns. Phillip takes his place behind one as well, as does Sarah. Her lectern is taller and placed in the center. All three face Autumn. The jurors now sit in a row off to one side.

Sarah Wellingsford gazes out from her raised position. Not surprisingly she's the first to speak. "We have gathered here tonight to determine the possible culpability of one of our own—a witch named Autumn Winters—with regard to the senseless murder of multiple vampires."

It's not lost on me that Sarah portrays Autumn as being "one of our own." After all, she's more likely to get what she wants if she appears to be impartial. Feeling me squirm in my seat, Phoenix squeezes my hand as Sarah continues.

"As you all know, a truce between supernatural factions has been holding for some time. An act such as this threatens that peace, and the perpetrator must be held responsible."

In other words, a few months ago it would have been fine to take out a few vampires. If anything, it would have been cause for celebration. But, hey, why not fuck over a veil witch if given the chance?

Thankfully, Phoenix gently squeezes my hand again just as I feel an involuntary surge of magic. This place may be warded, but I'm not sure they got their safeguards properly calibrated for my level of anger. Then again, that magic I feel is directed entirely at Sarah. Strange. What is it about her that would draw out my veil witch magic, especially when it's supposed to be nulled?

Still, this isn't a time to let my mind wander. I need to pay attention, and I force myself to focus when Sarah speaks again.

"In keeping with our coven traditions," she says, "the defendant has had her powers bound. Tonight we will determine whether her powers should be restored, or if"— Sarah pauses for dramatic effect as she looks around the room—"the defendant should suffer the punishment deemed appropriate for her crimes."

I want to strangle that bitch for the way she just reduced my sister to "the defendant," turning her into more of a thing than a person. Not to mention referring to those murders as "her crimes." Naturally, she also skipped the part about the punishment involving possibly being torn apart, or being essentially turned into a vampire slave.

Of course, Sarah's not done. In fact, I could swear she's enjoying the attention as she gazes around the room once more. "Since it has been some time since we were last forced to conduct such proceedings, allow me to explain the protocol. It is a simple one, without the pretenses and formalities of those observed by our non-magical counterparts. We will examine the evidence as presented by both parties. The arch vampire, Phillip, will speak for the aggrieved faction of our community. Isabel Aimes will speak for the accused. The defendant may speak too, at any time she wishes. Once the facts have been brought to light, the jury will be called upon to make a decision. The main difference in a trial such as this is that we are required to consider supernatural circumstances. Which we must accept are often quite nuanced."

Which I take to mean impossible to prove. Handy when you're trying to set someone up.

"If there are no questions," Sarah says, "we will begin the proceedings."

Sure, I have a question. How would you like me to tear your face off?

Apparently, I'm the only one with a question since, after surveying the room once more, Sarah turns her attention to the arch vampire. "Phillip, please tell us how you came to be informed of the crime."

From behind his lectern, Phillip glances out at the observers. Then he angles toward Sarah. "We learned about the murders from a member of the Vamanec P'yrin clan named Ellis. As some of you know, the Vamanec P'yrin can sense when there's been a breach in the veil. For reasons not made known to me, Ellis decided to visit the location of the disturbance. There, he came upon the crime scene."

A murmur ripples through the crowd, suggesting that many don't know of this ability possessed by the Vamanec P'yrin. Then again, that's not entirely surprising. Of those in the supernatural community, the Vamanec P'yrin remain the most reclusive and mysterious.

"Please tell us what happened next," Sarah says.

Phillip nods. "Ellis encountered one survivor, to whom he offered protection. Following that, he informed me about the incident. I dispatched a team to investigate."

Sarah reaches for a glass of water, taking the tiniest of sips. Almost like the glass is more a prop than something required for her thirst. "Can you tell us about this team?" she says, clearly suggesting that the request is at Phillip's discretion.

"Not their identities, of course. However, these individuals have a great deal of experience in examining supernatural crime scenes."

"Experts in magical forensics," Sarah offers.

"Yes. As well as making arrangements to obscure the occurrence of such events."

So, cleaners, basically. Obviously, had the police gotten involved to discover bodies reduced to ash, bone and advanced decomposition, they would have had a whole lot of questions. Phillip's team prevented that from happening.

"What kinds of details did this team report back to you?" Sarah asks.

"The house had been forcibly entered," Phillip says. "No doubt by supernatural means."

"Can you offer any specifics?"

Once again, Phillip nods. "The perpetrator used witch magic, definitely. The door, which had been secured, no longer had a locking mechanism. It had been melted in what could only have been an instance of extreme and precisely focused heat."

Sarah lets that resonate for a moment. "What, if anything, ruled out that having been done by a member of a different supernatural faction? Or, for that matter, at the hands of our non-magical counterparts?"

Wait, did Sarah just suggest it could have done by someone other than Autumn? I have my doubts, which are quickly confirmed when Phillip responds.

"A number of things, actually. The door itself was unmarked and undamaged, the lock, as I said, liquefied. While a vampire or werewolf could easily rip a door from its hinges, that wasn't the case. Also, there is no human technology allowing for what we observed."

"I see," Sarah says. "You felt sure it happened through witch magic. Was there anything suggesting a specific kind of witch?"

I brace myself, but Phillip shakes his head. "No. To the best of my knowledge, many witches could utilize this kind of magic. Most commonly, perhaps, elemental witches, but we couldn't be sure."

Another buzz comes from the crowd, as those gathered comment on what Phillip just said. Sarah seems not to notice, keeping her focus on Phillip as she stands almost perfectly still. For that matter, Phillip's posture is similarly immobile. For a vampire, that's not unusual, since they rarely shift on their feet or fidget. On the other hand, Sarah is said to be at least eighty and she shows no sign of fatigue.

My concentration breaks when Sarah says, "What else can you tell us about the crime scene?"

"There were almost no signs of struggle," Phillip says. "This suggested that the events must have transpired quickly."

"Did you consider that unusual?"

Phillip lifts an eyebrow. "Extremely."

"Why was that?"

Phillip looks out at us this time, as if to make sure we're paying attention. "As I'm sure you know, vampires are capable of reacting quite rapidly. However, in this instance, the victims appeared to have been immediately overwhelmed."

"And they weren't discovered to have been in a state of repose."

Sarah's formal phrasing indicates the sensitivity of the subject. Naturally, vampires don't like talking about the one state that leaves them completely vulnerable. In other words, when they're asleep. Dawn had been approaching fast, which would have left them supernaturally comatose until nightfall.

"That's correct," Phillip says. "Every sign indicated that they were awake at the time. Meaning, someone not only entered a house occupied by four vampires, but also managed to quickly kill them."

Okay, here we go. I feel certain that this is where Sarah will go in for the kill.

Sure enough, she says, "Please tell us about the state of the bodies."

Phillip shifts his attention to Autumn for the first time. She doesn't look away. Instead, she keeps her gaze fixed firmly on his.

"Essentially dust and bone," Phillip says. "There was very little left of the victims."

"And again for the record," Sarah says. "You felt sure the victims died at the hand of witch magic."

Phillip doesn't hesitate. "Absolutely."

"And did you eventually surmise what kind of witch?"

Phillip remains staring at Autumn. "Yes, based on several key elements. First, the crime was first discovered by someone who'd gone to investigate a breach in the veil. And, as I've explained, multiple victims were overwhelmed and reduced to a state of decomposition commensurate with what would have been their corresponding human age. Again, this appeared to have happened within a matter of minutes. Therefore, we felt entirely sure the crime could only have been committed by a veil witch."

As the crowd reacts, conversation rising through the room, Sarah raises her voice to be heard. "Of which we have only two," she says.

"That's my understanding," Phillip says. "Both of them sisters, one of whom had an ironclad alibi."

The hubbub around me continues to grow more loud, during which I hear both Autumn's name and mine repeatedly mentioned. The crowd starts to grow quiet again when Sarah raises her hand.

"Thank you, Phillip," she says, and then turns her attention to Isabel, who stands to her other side. "Isabel, you have offered to represent the defendant tonight. You're also doing this of your own free will."

Oh, my God, I want to murder this bitch. The implication being what? That one of us might have placed her under a spell? Given that Autumn doesn't currently have powers, the question barely makes sense. Although it still somehow manages to cast a nefarious light, which I suppose is Sarah's intention.

"I'm under my own free will," Isabel says. "Autumn is a friend of mine."

Sarah nods. "I see," she says, the simple phrase laden with unspoken suspicion. "You may proceed in the manner you best see fit."

Hang on. Let me get this right. After nearly leading the first testimony from beginning to end, she intends to let Isabel wing it? Apparently, that's the case. Fuck this supernatural trial bullshit. Sensing my growing rage, Phoenix tries again to help me calm down. It doesn't come close to working.

Still, somehow Isabel remains composed. She even manages to say, "Thank you," before turning to Autumn, upon whom she softly smiles. She hesitates for just a moment as she draws in a breath. Then she says, "Autumn, please tell us where you were that evening."

Considering the fate she's facing, Autumn looks remarkably poised. She calmly states, "Earlier, I was returning from the beach. After that, I stopped to see a friend at a bar. Then I went home, where I remained until morning."

"What time did you get home?"

"Around eleven-thirty."

Isabel nods. "It's been noted that you typically attend coven meetings, but that night you didn't. Why was that?"

I know what Isabel is doing with the question. People within the witch community have been talking about Autumn not attending the meeting that night. In most ways, that's completely irrelevant, but it still shows a departure from her usual behavior. For that reason, Isabel can't simply ignore it.

"I was weighing a personal decision," Autumn says.

"Which involved you thinking about your recently deceased husband." Isabel speaks softly, her tone sympathetic, but her voice still carries enough to be heard.

Autumn nods. "Yes. I needed some time alone."

Another soft murmur of conversation follows, presumably because so many people don't know that Autumn lost her husband. While I know Autumn was hesitant to discuss this part publicly, it still helps to show her in a sympathetic light.

Isabel looks out at the observers, and those still speaking fall silent. She turns back to Autumn. "As you stated, after you got home, you stayed home. Obviously, at some point while you slept, four vampires were murdered. Were you in any way involved in that crime?"

"I was not," Autumn says.

"Did you know any of the victims?"

Autumn shakes her head. "I didn't know them."

"So, you had nothing against them."

Autumn speaks calmly and evenly. "No, I had nothing against them."

Isabel considers for a moment. "And yet you're a veil witch. Aren't you supposed to hate vampires?"

Another good move by Isabel, calling attention to the elephant in the room. It wouldn't have surprised me if Sarah interrupted to make the same point.

Again, Autumn answers calmly. "We're not predisposed to hating anyone. Veil witches simply have the power to remove supernatural threats."

"I see," Isabel says. "So, you wouldn't break into a house where vampires lived and kill them for no reason."

Isabel poses this as a statement, not a question. By doing so, she makes the idea seem ludicrous.

"Of course not," Autumn says.

"As you stated earlier, when you got home you stayed home. When did you next leave your apartment?"

"Early the next morning, I woke up to find that I'd been taken."

Isabel frowns. "Taken where?"

Autumn shakes her head. "I don't know. I was in a dark room lit by flames floating near the ceiling."

Isabel glances up to the ceiling of the atrium. "Like those flames?"

Autumn nods. "Yes. Flames without candles, clearly created by magic."

The observers all look up, of course, then back to the dais again when Isabel next speaks.

"Who took you there?"

Again, Autumn shakes her head. "I don't know. They were wearing masks."

Isabel raises her eyebrows. "Let me make sure I understand. You were somehow transported from your home to another location. When you woke up, those surrounding you wore masks."

How Autumn holds it together is beyond me, but she simply says, "Yes, that's the case."

"Please tell us what happened next."

"I was held bound. They took my blood and cast a spell removing my magic. Then they blew a powder in my face. That's the last thing I remember before I found myself back home again."

Autumn's words produce way more than a murmur in the crowd this time, as conversation openly breaks out and voices rise. I hear surprise, indignation and confusion in the comments of those around me. Nice, Isabel. Very nice. After all, bindings are very rare, so presumably the methods involved aren't often brought to light.

My eyes go to where Sarah stands at her lectern, somehow maintaining her impassive expression. Apparently, she considered it within her rights to do what she did, but it seems evident that many around us feel differently, even despite their prejudice against veil witches.

This time, it's Isabel who holds up her hand to quiet the room. Then she shifts her attention back to Autumn.

"So, you were detained by witches who didn't identify themselves. Were you ever given the chance to submit for questioning of your own free will?"

Despite the humiliation she suffered, Autumn still manages to hold her head high. "No. I was not given that chance."

Isabel turns from Autumn to the jury. "It seems to me we might need to later revisit whether any other crimes occurred during the course of these events. If not magical crimes, certainly criminal offenses. Clearly, Autumn Winter's rights were violated in a number of ways. But that's for us to determine later. Right now, it's for you to decide whether Autumn should be found guilty of the crimes for which she's been accused. As you can see, there's no reason to think so. She didn't know the victims, had no quarrels with them, and there's no clear evidence connecting her to their murders."

Sarah, who has remained silent this whole time, finally speaks again. "So, you're saying you can't offer any evidence supporting the defendant's claim?"

"We have her word," Isabel says.

Sarah lifts an eyebrow. "We have her *word*? Why would that possibly be good enough?"

Isabel cocks her head, suggesting that Sarah isn't making sense. "Why wouldn't it be? Autumn Winters is a valued member of our community. Not only has she never caused any of us harm, she's protected us on a number of occasions. You've presented no solid evidence linking her to the crime. Essentially, you're asking the jury to take your word regarding a matter you didn't witness, following which you took the law into your own hands."

Sarah's eyes light up with fury, even as she manages to still speak calmly. In fact, a small satisfied smile remains on her face. "You seem to be forgetting one key element. Those who were *murdered*, met their fate at the hands of a veil witch. We have only two in our community. No one else possesses these kinds of powers. Of the two, one was at the coven meeting and then later seen in the company of her fellow witches. On the other hand, the defendant claims to have been home asleep."

Isabel considers for a moment. "So, what you're saying is that if I could offer evidence of there being a third veil witch, this case would have to be dismissed."

Sarah hesitates, her eyes tightening as her gaze bores into Isabel. Then she says, "Can you offer such evidence?"

"I can't," Isabel says.

Sarah's smile widens into a grin. For a few moments time seems to stop, the room around us utterly silent.

Then Isabel speaks again. "Perhaps we should ask those around us here tonight. Would that be okay with you?"

Sarah's face tightens more, her eyes suspicious. All the same, what choice does she have? "Of course," she says. "Although, I can't imagine—"

"Over here!" I say, rising to my feet. "I might have something."

Sarah's eyes meet mine, amusement showing in her superior gaze. "And you'd expect us to believe you?"

I shake my head. "Me, no. You hate veil witches, obviously. At least me and my sister. What I'm thinking is that we hear from some of our most bitter enemies."

Then Sarah stares, her mouth dropping open, as at the back of the room John, Eric, Stephanie and Nora rise from their seats. When I thought they'd fled last night, that hadn't been the case. Even though they could have easily died, Nora convinced them to stay in case they could help. Now they approach the dais where, one by one, they each tell their story so those gathered here will know what they witnessed.

As Sarah Wellingsford's credibility crumbles in front the witch community, I keep wondering about that magic I still feel simmering within me. I'm beyond curious, but I guess it will have to wait. And when the jurors announce Autumn innocent, I look to my sister, who returns my gaze. Within her eyes, I see that same girl who once sat with me watching the Powerpuff Girls as we imagined ourselves future heroes. My big sister, who's always been there for me and always will be. Then my gaze goes to Isabel, who I know must be thinking of her daughter, and I start to plan my next steps.

The next book in the Fae Witch Chronicles
series will be out soon! Be the first to find out
by joining J.S. Malcom's Reader Group
www.jsmalcom.com

Author Note

I have to say, these books just keep getting more fun to write, and this fifth installment in the Fae Witch Chronicles series was no exception. When the idea of Cassie being forced to team up with a vampire first occurred to me, I knew I had to at least give it a try. There seemed to be so much potential for Cassie—our highly opinionated and impetuous hero—to grow when faced with an arrangement she'd normally avoid at all costs (or by simply reducing the vampire to a pile of bones). The result of this exploration in character development is this book which you, presumably, just finished reading. I hope enjoyed the adventure as much as I enjoyed creating it.

As always, I owe thanks to all who "beta-read" an earlier draft of this novel. I greatly appreciate your taking the time to share your thoughts, as well as helping to catch those edits that still needed to happen. Thank you to Carmen Repsold, Jennifer Mantura, Joe Estanelle, Jennifer Ryan, Deborah MacArthur, Marja Coons-Torn, Patti and Patrick Winters, Rachel Karfit, Lacey Lane, Lori Kis, Susan Warr, Andrea van der Westhuizen, Tammy Baker, Diane Changala, Tamara Ingram, Maria Mybeck, Jana Gundy, Joe Estanelle, Kim Brown, Jenine Hightower, Heather Price, Shauna Joesten, Jen Simmerman, Gretchen Bayard, Darcy Smith, Judith Cohen, Gary Webber and Vicki McCreary. Many thanks also to Kim, Darja and Milo at Deranged Doctor Design for creating such stunning book covers.

About J. S. Malcom

J. S. Malcom is the author of the Realm Watchers urban fantasy series, of which Autumn Winters is just the beginning. J. S. lives in Richmond, Virginia, a town full of history and ghosts (not to mention, many other supernatural creatures, including Autumn and Cassie).

Made in the USA
Monee, IL
10 February 2020